About the Author

Eleanor Agnes Berry is the author of 20 published books and says her first brush with literature was when she broke windows in Ian Fleming's house at the age of eight. 'He struck me as being a singularly disagreeable man, with no understanding of children,' she recalls. Of Welsh ancestry, she was born and bred in London. She holds a BA Hons degree (a 2:2) in English.

Eleanor specialises in black humour. The works of Gorki, Dostoevsky, Gogol, Edgar Allan Poe, James Hadley Chase, George Orwell and Joe Orton have strongly influenced her writings. While at university she completed an unpublished textual thesis on the Marquis de Sade (whom she refers to as 'de Soggins'). In her spare time she wrote a grossly indecent book, entitled *The Story of Paddy,* which she had the good sense to burn, and inadvertently set a garage on

After leaving university she worked as a commercial translator, using French and Russian. She then worked as research assistant to a Harley Street specialist and has also worked intermittently as a medical secretary. She was nearly sacked from St Bartholomew's Hospital in London because she had been a close friend of the late Robert Maxwell's. (She had worked there for five years!)

Two of her novels are available in Russian and a third, which she refrains from naming, is currently being made into a film. This is her eleventh book to be published by Guild Publishing.

Eleanor is the author of numerous articles in *The Oldie* magazine and has appeared on television and on radio several times, including Radio California. Her interests include Russian literature, Russian folk songs, Irish rebel songs, the cinema, amateur piano playing, sensational court cases, the medical profession, entertaining her nephews, and swimming across Marseilles harbour for kicks. When she dies, she will have her ashes scattered over Marseilles harbour, her favourite place.

Eleanor is the maternal niece of the late, famous, self-confessed gypsy author, Eleanor Smith, after whom she was named. Sadly, Eleanor Smith died before Eleanor was born.

Books by Eleanor Berry

Tell Us a Sick One Jakey (A black comedy about a mortuary attendant who dies of a brain tumour. Out of print.)
Never Alone with Rex Malone
Your Father Died on the Gallows (two editions) (available in Russian)
Someone's Been Done Up Harley
O, Hitman, My Hitman!
The Revenge of Miss Rhoda Buckleshott
The Most Singular Adventures of Eddy Vernon
Take It Away, It's Red!
Stop the Car, Mr Becket! (formerly *The Rendon Boy to the Grave Is Gone*)
Robert Maxwell as I Knew Him
Cap'n Bob and Me
McArandy was Hanged on the Gibbet High
The House of the Weird Doctors
Sixty Funny Stories
The Most Singular Adventures of Sarah Lloyd
Alandra Varinia – Sarah's Daughter
The Rise and Fall of Mad Silver Jaxton
By the Fat of Unborn Leopards
The Killing of Lucinda Maloney
My Old Pal was a Junkie (available in Russian)

Reviews

Tell Us a Sick One Jakey
'This book is quite repulsive!' Sir Michael Havers, Attorney General

Never Alone with Rex Malone
'A ribald, ambitious black comedy, a story powerfully told.' Stewart Steven, *The Daily Mail*

'I was absolutely flabbergasted when I read it!' Robert Maxwell

Your Father Died on the Gallows
'A unique display of black humour which somehow fails to depress the reader.' Craig McLittle, *The Rugby Gazette*

'This book is an unheard of example of English black humour. Eleanor Berry is almost a reincarnation of our own beloved Dostoevsky.' Sergei Robkov, Russian magazine, *Minuta*

Robert Maxwell as I Knew Him
'One of the most amusing books I have read for a long time. Eleanor Berry is an original.' Elisa Segrave, *The Literary Review*

'Undoubtedly the most amusing book I have read all year.' Julia Llewellyn-Smith, *The Times*

'With respect and I repeat, with very great respect, because

I know you're a lady, but all you ever do is just go on and on and on and on about this bleeding bloke,' Reginald Kray.

Cap'n Bob and Me
'A comic masterpiece.' *The Times*

'As befits the maternal granddaughter of F.E. Smith (famous barrister who never lost a case) Eleanor Berry has a sharp tone of phrase and a latent desire for upsetting people. Campaigning for her hero, Robert Maxwell, in a General Election, she climbed to the top of the Buckingham Town Hall with intent to erect the red flag. Eleanor fits into the long tradition of British eccentricity.' Stewart Graham, *The Spectator*

Someone's Been Done Up Harley
'In this book, Eleanor Berry's dazzling wit hits the Harley Street scene. Her extraordinary humour had me in stitches.' Thelma Masters, *The Oxford Times*

O, Hitman, My Hitman!
'Eleanor Berry's volatile pen is at it again. This time, she takes her readers back to the humorously eccentric Harley Street community. She also introduces Romany gypsies and travelling circuses, a trait which she has inherited from her self-confessed maternal gypsy aunt, the late writer, Eleanor Smith, after whom she was named. Like Smith, Berry is an inimitable and delightfully natural writer.' Kev Zein, *The Johannesburg Evening Sketch*

McArandy was Hanged on the Gibbet High
'We have here a potboiling, swashbuckling blockbuster, which is rich in adventure, intrigue, history, amorous episodes and black humour. The story Eleanor Berry tells is multi-coloured, multi-faceted and nothing short of fantastic.' Angel Z. Hogan, *The Daily Melbourne Times*

The Revenge of Miss Rhoda Buckleshott
'Words are Eleanor Berry's toys and her use of them is boundless.' Mary Hickman, professional historian and writer

The Most Singular Adventures of Eddy Vernon
'Rather a hot book for bedtime.' Nigel Dempster, *The Daily Mail*

Stop the Car, Mr Becket! (formerly *The Rendon Boy to the Grave is Gone*)
'This book makes for fascinating reading, as strange, black humoured and entertaining as Eleanor Berry's other books which came out before it.' Gaynor Evans, *The Bristol Evening Post*

Take it Away, It's Red!
'Despite the sometimes weighty portent of this book, a sense of subtle, dry and powerfully engaging humour reigns throughout its pages. The unexpected twist is stupendous.' Stephen Carson, *The Carolina Sun*

Sixty Funny Stories
'This book is a laugh a line.' Elisa Segrave, writer and diarist.

The House of the Weird Doctors
'This delightful medical caper puts even A.J. Cronin in the shade.' Noel I. Leskin, *The Stethoscope*

The Most Singular Adventures of Sarah Lloyd
'A riotous read from start to finish.' Ned McMurphy, *The Irish Times*

Alandra Varinia – Sarah's Daughter
'Eleanor Berry manages to maintain her raw and haunting wit as much as ever.' Dwight C. Farr, *The Texas Chronicle*

The Rise and Fall of Mad Silver Jaxton
'This time, Eleanor Berry tries her versatile hand at politics. Her sparkling wit and the reader's desire to turn the page are still in evidence. Eleanor Berry is unique.' Don F. Saunderson, *The South London Review*

'This is a dark, disturbing but at the same time hilarious tale of a megalomaniac dictator by the always readable and naughty Eleanor.' Sally Farmiloe, award-winning actress and author.

By the Fat of Unborn Leopards
'Could this ribald, grisly-humoured story about a British newspaper magnate's daughter, possibly be autobiographical, by any chance?' Peggy-Lou Kadinsky, *The Washington Globe*

'Fantastically black. A scream from beginning to end.' Charles Kidd, Editor of *Debrett's Peerage*

The Killing of Lucinda Maloney
'This is the funniest book I've read for months,' Samantha Morris, *The Exeter Daily News*

My Old Pal was a Junkie
'Eleanor Berry is to literature what Hieronymus Bosch is to art. As with all Miss Berry's books, the reader has a burning urge to turn the page.' Sonia Drew, *The International Continental Review*

MY OLD PAL WAS A JUNKIE

A JUNKIE

(A Black Comedy)

Eleanor Berry

www.eleanorberry.net

Book Guild Publishing

Sussex, England

First published in Great Britain in 2013 by
The Book Guild Ltd
The Werks
45 Church Road
Hove, BN3 2BE

Typesetting in Baskerville by
Keyboard Services, Luton, Bedfordshire

Printed in Great Britain by
CPI Antony Rowe

A catalogue record for this book is available from
The British Library

ISBN 978 1 84624 889 4

For my sister, Harriet

It was a Friday evening on the fifteenth of March in the late nineteen seventies.

In a caravan, at an upright piano, sat a thirty-five-year-old woman who was playing the last movement of a concerto of her own composition. Her caravan was parked on a caravan site in Berkshire, near Reading, about forty miles west of London.

In a corner of the caravan was an unemptied bucket which the woman used as a lavatory. In another corner was a harp. In a third corner was a screen behind which was a narrow unmade bed, which had no sheets – only a pile of filthy blankets. There was a gas heater near the bed. There was a long table and two or three chairs in the caravan. On the table, among other things, was a guitar, a pile of handwritten sheets of music, which were also of the woman's own composition, and a bowl of cold water which she used for washing her face in.

The woman did not look as if she were only thirty-five years old. She was five foot seven inches tall and weighed about six stone. She had long, unwashed, waist-length jet-black hair and a distinctly feline face, almost like a cat's. Her large grey eyes were sunken like a skull's, and bloodshot, due to alcohol and drug abuse. Her teeth were blackened and her breath stank of stale gin.

1

The last movement of her concerto was similar in places to a Russian folk song, in that the music started slowly and mournfully and gradually gathered speed.

She had on a pair of tattered blue jeans, a thick navy blue polo-necked sweater, a worn out black leather jacket, filthy training shoes and a pair of unwashed socks. At her feet lay a golden Labrador which, unlike its mistress, was glossy and well-nourished.

The woman suddenly felt the cramps of substance withdrawal coming on. She stopped playing the piano abruptly and clutched her stomach. She hastily took some white powder wrapped up in silver foil from the table, emptied it into a dessert spoon and added water to it which she took from the bowl. She heated the spoon from underneath it with a cigarette lighter. She then pulled down her jeans and drew the substance, which was heroin, into a syringe and injected it into her groin.

Her cramps immediately disappeared but she no longer experienced the euphoria that she had enjoyed when she had first started to use heroin. She left the score of her last concerto in the piano rack, stared despairingly into space and started to walk towards the door of the caravan. She had a pronounced limp because she had given herself so many heroin injections in one of her legs that many of her muscles had wasted away, and hence her gait was lurching and masculine.

The golden Labrador moved across her path and whined piteously, raising its front right paw in a begging position. It knew that its owner would not be returning to the caravan. The woman caressed the dog and disappeared into the night, oblivious of the weather, which was wet, windy and cold. She didn't care about the welfare of the dog which she had left behind.

She walked for about two miles though the fields until she reached a bridge over the M4 motorway which was full of traffic leaving London. She climbed over the railings and sat on the edge of the bridge, waiting for a vehicle moving fast enough to kill her.

* * *

Marcia Ford lived in London and was happy and prosperous. She was thirty-five years old but she looked much younger than her years. She had recently started a job, working as a sub-editor on the *Daily Mail*. She had driven out of London and was on her way to her second house in Bath where she planned to stay for the weekend. She was driving a British racing green BMW in the left lane of the motorway, as the traffic in the central lane and the outside lane was moving particularly slowly.

Marcia had been graced with good looks. Her hair was red, and cut short. She had a fringe and her eyes were a Caribbean shade of blue. She was five foot five inches tall and weighed about nine stone.

She had on a bottle green velvet suit, a white cashmere sweater, a gold pendant round her neck and high-heeled green suede shoes which matched her suit. She had draped a bottle green, fur-lined raincoat, purchased from Harrods, in the back of her BMW. Bottle green was her favourite colour.

She put on a cassette of Handel's Saraband Duo in D minor. Its slow and haunting tones had a rousing and hypnotic effect on her. She increased her speed and laughed with joy.

Suddenly, she felt something hit her. She swerved onto the hard shoulder and screeched to a halt. She saw a woman lying in the left lane of the motorway, and her initial reaction was that of fear that she had killed her. She was tempted to drive on but she was law-abiding and decided to get out of her car. The woman was not seriously hurt and staggered to her feet. She just managed to walk onto the hard shoulder and leant over the bonnet of the car.

'What the bloody hell do you think you're doing?' shouted Marcia. Her voice was loud, deep and commanding and her accent educated. The other woman did not answer and continued to lean against the car, breathing heavily.

'Get in the car!' shouted Marcia, adding, 'are you badly hurt?'

The woman did as she was told. She muttered that she was not badly hurt.

Marcia engaged gear and pulled out. She looked briefly at her emaciated passenger's profile and markedly feline face, which for some reason troubled her, as if she had seen her somewhere before and could not remember where. The cassette no longer caused her the sense of well-being that it had before she had been intruded upon. She felt the conflicting emotions of confusion and irritation and spoke with a clipped military bark.

'Next time you wish to commit suicide, you might at

least do so in the privacy of your bathroom. All you would lose would be your life. I could have lost my driving licence.'

'I haven't got a bathroom,' the woman replied. Her voice was shrill with a marked lisp and a flat regional brogue. Apart from her accent, which she had gained later on in her life, her voice was alarmingly familiar. Marcia swerved onto the hard shoulder and screeched to a halt a second time.

'Jess!' she exclaimed in an astounded tone, 'Jessie Cavendish, the girl who was nicknamed "Cat Face" at school!'

The woman didn't answer and leant forward, looking at the floor of the car.

'Don't you remember me? We were at school together. You were one of my closest friends,' said Marcia.

'I've done everything in my power to forget those days,' said Jessie.

'I've got happy memories of that school. I think the thing I valued most was the camaraderie of the other girls.'

'You'd be happy anywhere because you are an idiot,' said Jessie sullenly.

A long silence ensued. Jessie continued to look at the floor of the car and Marcia looked at the unfolding motorway, hurt by her companion's words.

'What happened to you since you left school?' asked Marcia eventually.

'I won a scholarship to the Royal Academy of Music in London. I was thrown out because I was away a lot of the time. I married a Scotsman called Malcolm Lowther and had a child by him, a son. I left my husband because I came home one day and found him in bed with another man. I was drinking heavily at the time as well as using heroin, and a few years later, my son, aged seven, was taken into care, although I had stopped using heroin when he was born. I might never see him again. I wouldn't have minded so much if I'd had a family of my own. My son is the only blood relation I've got. You're lucky – you come from a large family.' (Marcia's parents were still alive. She had two brothers and a sister, as well as five nephews to whom she was devoted.)

'I'm so sorry to hear your news, Cat Face. You've had a lot of bad luck but are you convinced that you actually want to kill yourself?' asked Marcia kindly.

'What have I got to live for?'

'You've got quite a lot to live for. You are a highly talented musician who might one day become internationally famous. When your son is old enough, you may be reunited with him.'

'Every day of my life is intolerable. I'm not prepared to wait that long,' said Jessie in a deadpan tone of voice.

Marcia thought for a while before saying anything.

'All right. I'll make a pact with you. On Monday morning, I'll take you to the Clifton Suspension Bridge in Bristol where there is a two hundred and forty-five foot drop. If you climb over the safety barrier, you'll be dead in a matter of seconds. I warn you, the safety barrier is extremely difficult to climb over. But first, I'll take you back to London where I'll give you the best weekend of your life. We'll do

6

anything you want. I'll phone my work number on Monday morning and say I've got a heavy cold.'

'Who told you the exact depth of the bridge's drop?' asked Jessie, her tone partly mocking and partly curious.

'Oh, it's just something I happen to know,' answered Marcia, adding, 'I can't remember who told me.'

When Jessie understood that she would shortly be taken to a place to die, she cheered up a little.

'Well, you've heard about me. Tell me about yourself. What happened to you since you left that ghastly school? Are you still a starry-eyed communist?' she asked.

'A communist?' Marcia laughed raucously. 'I gave all that up when I went behind the Iron Curtain. When I found out what communism was really like, I had a nervous breakdown.' A sudden note of bitterness came into her voice. ' "We'll build gold latrines for the workers," ' Lenin* had promised in his manifesto. I took his words very seriously. I went to a public lavatory in Moscow and I expected it to be made of solid gold. It was quite the most disgusting lavatory I'd ever seen and when I pulled the chain, it came away in my hand and the cistern crashed to the floor.'

Jessie gave an extraordinarily shrill, neighing laugh which started on a high note and gradually went down the scale. Throughout her life, her laugh was the only feature which readily endeared her to others.

'Do you mean you had a nervous breakdown just because the chain came away in your hand when you pulled it?' she asked.

*Leader of the Bolshevik Party and revered founder of the Soviet State.

7

'It's what the whole thing represented that finished me off. I had really believed in communism and when that happened my whole belief was shattered.'

The two women suddenly had hysterical giggles. Marcia's laughter was nervous but essentially joyful. Jessie's was joyless.

Marcia followed the sign to Reading and turned off the motorway. She turned her BMW round and headed for London.

* * *

It was at Waltham Abbey, a public school in Buckinghamshire, where Marcia and Jessie first met at the beginning of the autumn term in the early nineteen sixties. Waltham Abbey was a strict, academically-renowned Protestant boarding school of neo-Gothic architecture with gaunt imposing outside walls which were a dark shade of grey. The school's highly formidable headmistress, Miss Hermione Heathcote-Barrow, was forty-two years old and was the daughter of the late Horatio Heathcote-Barrow, who had been the Archbishop of Canterbury until he retired. Miss Heathcote-Barrow had grey hair, streaked with white, beady brown eyes, prominent cheekbones and a sallow complexion. The school had a chapel attached to it, which it was compulsory to attend once a day, and twice a day on Sundays.

Marcia and Jessie were both thirteen years old when they first met. Jessie was the tallest of the two. At that time, Jessie, who had a distinctly feline face, had a mane of thick, well-brushed, jet-black hair, swept back from her face in a slide, and melancholy, large grey eyes. Her hair reached her waist. She was striking rather than pretty. Marcia's red hair was arranged in a single plait. Even at the age of thirteen, she was exceptionally pretty.

The two girls were sitting next to each other during one of the chapel services one Sunday. A parson was giving a rambling and uninteresting sermon with the unoriginal theme of venereal disease being divine punishment for sin. Jessie was engrossed in composing a piece of music.

'Do you write music?' Marcia asked in a whisper.

'Looks like it, doesn't it?' Jessie said and went on writing.

'Sorry I asked.'

'Pity you did.'

Marcia's admiration for Jessie's ability to write music and for her quickness of tongue conflicted with a feeling of humiliation. She wondered whether to befriend her but decided to ignore her for fear of being humiliated further.

Later on that day, was a ceremony known as 'house order'. In each house, and in Marcia's and Jessie's case, Churchill House, everyone assembled in a circle in order of seniority while the housemistress, Miss Mildred Armstrong, complained bitterly about the girls who stood before her.

Mildred Armstrong was unhappy. She had been jilted in her twenties and had never married. She was ten years older than Miss Heathcote-Barrow. Miss Heathcote-Barrow had been the headmistress of Waltham Abbey for ten years, whereas Miss Armstrong had been the housemistress of Churchill House for eight years. Before that, she had worked as a matron in an institution for incontinent boys but had been dismissed because she had subjected them to amateur psychoanalysis, an unpleasant habit which she indulged in, even when she became the house-mistress of Churchill House. In her early life, she had worked as a missionary in Nigeria but she had been swiftly relieved of her responsibilities for reasons which were never disclosed. Whenever she was baffled or angry, she had an extremely bizarre habit of uttering the words 'Heigh-ho'.

Her profile was her only feature which suggested that she had been pretty in her youth. She had a small, straight nose but her pale blue eyes were staring and Hitlerian. Her grey hair was cropped close to her head. Her clothes were shabby and ill-fitting, and purchased from Oxfam shops, and her voice was deep and gruff.

As she entered the room, known as the 'house study', the girls stood to attention and some of them straightened their collars and ties. (The girls also did their prep in the house study.)

'Last term,' Miss Armstrong began, 'Churchill House had a reputation for being disgustingly slack. If I notice any recurrence of this despicable and irresponsible lack of team spirit among any of you, I shall come *crashing* down on offenders.'

She punched the palm of her left hand with her right fist as she spoke. One of the girls got the giggles, but stopped giggling when her eyes met the livid glare of the head of house, Hilda Swain, who had played a hackneyed and genteel Hamlet the term before. She was permanently pursued by sycophantic juniors who had crushes on her and who asked her for her autograph.

'A slackness of attitude very often stems from personal slovenliness and lack of moral fibre,' continued Miss Armstrong. 'This morning, I happened to go into the bootroom.' (A room where coats, hats, shoes, lacrosse sticks and lockers were kept and which was referred to by the girls as the 'booter'. The girls went there for their elevenses.)

Miss Armstrong added, 'Heigh-ho, to my disgust, I noticed that someone had upset a pot of tea over one of the tables. Tea was actually *seeping* through a crack in the table and was dripping onto the floor. It was a vile and sickening sight, sickening because it reflected the casual, slap-happy mentality of the sluts responsible. Heigh-ho, I don't think on going into the bootrooms in any of the other houses that I would be subjected to anything as sickening and degrading as the sight of tea *seeping*,' (she laid a strong emphasis on the word 'seeping') 'through a crack in a table.'

Marcia had been at the school for a year. She was standing next to Jessie who was new that term. Suddenly, Jessie collapsed in helpless giggles. Marcia caught them like a virus and laughed out loud.

'Marcia Ford and Jessie Cavendish, you appear to find sluttishness funny,' shrieked Miss Armstrong, now in a thunderous rage. 'Heigh-ho, you had better both come and see me in my study.'

Miss Armstrong's study was large and airy. It had white walls, a beige carpet and armchairs covered with pale blue cloth. In a corner of the room by the window was a small table supported by elephants' tusks on which lay an empty and meticulously polished ashtray. A log fire burned in the grate. On the mantelpiece was a photograph of the staff and pupils at the institution for incontinent boys with Miss Armstrong sitting in the centre, holding a silver cup, smiling with ruthless determination.

Miss Armstrong stood with her back to the fire, facing Marcia and Jessie. Jessie looked bored and cynical. Marcia looked frightened. She had every reason to be frightened of Miss Armstrong. The previous term, the hysterical, masculine-looking housemistress had rounded up girls whom she considered to be eccentric and subjected them to alarming, deep-rooted psychoanalysis. Among them was Marcia Ford. She summoned the thirteen-year-old girl to her study at eleven o'clock one night, having woken her up.

'How close are you to your father?' the housemistress asked, in an interfering tone of voice.

'My father sleeps in the basement and I sleep on the second floor. To reach that distance from outside the house, a crow would have to fly about twenty-eight feet,' replied Marcia, in a deadpan tone of voice.

Miss Armstrong hadn't expected Marcia's bold answer which she considered impertinent and punished her by making her forfeit one of her weekend outings that term.

When Jessie and Marcia were summoned to Miss Armstrong's study together the following term, the housemistress began her reprimand with the words, 'Heigh-ho, I need hardly tell you both why you are here.' She directed her stare at Jessie rather than Marcia. Jessie stared straight ahead defiantly and failed to look Miss Armstrong in the eye. The housemistress continued to stare at Jessie. 'From someone of *your* background, I would expect such a dastardly sense of comedy in reacting to the hateful and the revolting. In one born, bred and raised by riffraff, you are actually privileged to attend this school, Jessie Cavendish.'

Miss Armstrong turned her glare to Marcia and said, 'On the other hand, with someone of your background and lofty social lineage, I am nothing short of appalled that you should sink to such depths and laugh so inappropriately.' (Marcia's father was a wealthy, well-known newspaper magnate. His name was Sir William Ford. He was the Chairman and Editor-in-Chief of *The London Globe* and *The Sunday Bulletin*. These were both Conservative newspapers.)

Jessie stopped staring straight ahead and stared insolently at Miss Armstrong. Marcia admired her but was too frightened to copy her. She looked briefly at the flames that flickered in the grate and finally looked Miss Armstrong in the eye, looking guilty and compliant.

'Heigh-ho, you come from a literary background and a highly respectable newspaper family, Marcia Ford, and yet you find the idea of tea seeping through a crack in a table funny.'

It was obvious that Miss Armstrong was becoming bored with the situation.

'Heigh-ho, if either of you is impertinent again, you will be appropriately punished and punished very severely. Now, get out, the pair of you, before I change my mind and decide to punish you now.'

Marcia and Jessie left the room and walked in silence downstairs, out onto the drive. Suddenly, Jessie threw her arms round Marcia and sobbed uncontrollably. Marcia was delighted to have made friends with this bold, proud and talented girl with the delightfully feline face. She too began to weep, but unlike those of her new friend, hers were tears of joy.

'Tell me, Jessie,' Marcia began, 'what did Miss Armstrong mean when she said that your background was riffraff?'

'People I like call me Cat Face, not Jessie,' said Jessie, adding, 'that includes you, Marcia.'

The two girls sat down on a wooden seat in the drive, outside Churchill House. It was a chilly, bleak September day and the wind and dead leaves whistled about them. Jessie then told Marcia the story of her early life.

* * *

The year was nineteen fifty-six. Lazlo Zartak, a talented Hungarian musician, but crooked gypsy fortune-teller of no fixed abode, had camped his caravan on a piece of land in western Hungary, which was interspersed with hills and woods. (He hailed from eastern Hungary.) Zartak was one of the last of a long line of cut-throats and thieves. There were no graveyards in the part of the world that his forefathers had come from. The dead had been either murdered or hanged and the vultures had eaten their corpses from the gallows.

Zartak was in his twenties. He was well-built with jet black hair, large grey eyes and a feline face like his daughter's. His old caravan had belonged to his grandfather, Zoltan, and had been acquired after a feud. Zoltan and a group of thugs had murdered its former occupants with peculiarly revolting cruelty. The caravan was towed by a stolen cart horse and as Zartak permanently broke the law, he seldom remained in one place for more than two days at a time.

His wife, Maria, had left him for another rootless wanderer. When Zartak had stabbed his rival to death in a brawl, Maria grew terrified of her violent husband and travelled to the nearest town where she found work as a washerwoman.

Zartak's only living blood relation was his five-year-old daughter, Rosa,* on whom he doted. She had inherited her father's jet black hair and large grey eyes. She had witnessed the killing of her father's rival and had developed an obsessive dependence on her father, fearing that he would abandon her one day. She had never particularly liked her mother, because she had been unfaithful to her father.

* * *

The Russians invaded Hungary on the fourth of November, nineteen fifty-six. One evening, as Zartak was playing one of his compositions to Rosa on his accordion, a truck occupied by Russian militiamen approached his caravan. Zartak and his daughter were staying near a hamlet called Krannat. The Zartaks were forced by the Russian militiamen

*Later to be known as Jessie Cavendish and nick-named 'Cat Face' by those whom she liked.

15

to abandon their caravan and move to the nearest town, where Zartak was allocated a job repairing pot holes in the streets and was given a damp basement room on the outskirts of the town. Rosa was put in a crèche during the day but she failed to get on with the other children because she was rude and unfriendly. In the evenings, Zartak and his daughter shared the sordid basement room with the Weillands, another family.

Russian tanks rumbled like crocodiles through Hungary. Living conditions in the basement room were cramped. A single sink, running cold water only, served as a bath in the room which was used as a kitchen, a bedroom, a dining-room and a lavatory. There was a slop bucket in one corner of the room.

Zartak shared anti-Soviet sentiments with the Weillands who introduced him to contacts enabling him to get forged passports for him and his daughter to escape to Austria. The rebel camaraderie was short-lived, however. Zartak's foul temper, due to his hideous living conditions, led to bitter quarrels between the two families.

Joseph Weilland was the head of the Weilland family. He was a teacher and a practising anti-Soviet agitator. His wife, Anna, was a librarian and a distributor of anti-Soviet leaflets. Their son, Daniel, had been imprisoned for preaching anti-Soviet propaganda to crowds in the streets.

Joseph and Anna disappeared one day and never returned to the dirty room. Zartak, who had arranged to get forged passports for him and his daughter, decided that it was time to move out of the room and find his way back to his caravan.

It was then early February, nineteen fifty-seven. After a terrifying escape through the rat-infested sewers of the tank-infested town, Zartak and Rosa returned to the area near the hamlet, Krannat, where their caravan had been abandoned. They found the caravan on its side with the body of their faithful but stolen cart horse lying beside it. The horse's body had been eaten to the bones by carrion birds. With a great effort, Zartak pushed the caravan upright. The father and daughter stayed in the caravan for a few days. It was bitterly cold and it was snowing heavily with blizzards. They hugged each other tightly, in order to keep warm.

One morning, the Zartaks came out of their caravan and Zartak saw an elderly peasant driving a horse and cart along a dirt track. He stood in front of the horse, blocking its path.

'Where are you going?' he called out.

'Budapest. My sister's dying.'

'Budapest? Don't you know it's under siege? The Russians invaded the whole country last November. Besides, it's miles away from here.'

'What do you mean, Budapest's under siege?'

'The Russians invaded the city three months ago. They're occupying the whole country, as I said. Didn't you know that?'

Zartak was afraid that the peasant would report him to someone, so he climbed onto his cart and hit him repeatedly over the head with a hammer, killing him outright. Also, he needed his horse to tow his caravan.

'Did you kill that man?' asked Rosa inanely.

'It looks like it, doesn't it?'

'He's not the only man you've killed, is he?'

'Sometimes, it is necessary to kill in order to survive. There are times when you have to steal and lie to survive as well. It's not wrong to do any of these things, although certain rules say otherwise,' said Zartak, adding, 'we're taking the caravan to a hamlet called Tusenbak which is close to the Austrian border where there are frontier guards. There is a dense wood at the frontier. I've managed to get two forged passports. Hopefully, the guards will find them in order. Then we'll cross the border and go to Austria where we'll be able to live as we like.'

The Zartaks travelled along a narrow road through a dense wood. Rosa was unaware of the danger ahead and wished she could go on travelling with her father forever.

The Zartaks drove deeper into the wood and came to a halt. They had almost reached the hamlet, Tusenbak. They got out of their caravan and sat down at the edge of the narrow, bumpy road. Zartak wrenched some branches off a tree and built up a fire.

He then managed to catch a rabbit which he skinned and cooked on the fire. He shared it with Rosa. When the father and daughter had finished eating their meagre fare, Zartak took a strange looking knife from his belt. The blade of the knife was about a foot long and it had an ornate ivory handle.

As Zartak held the knife in front of the fire, Rosa saw that its blade was covered with words in tiny Gothic letters.

'This is the famous Zartak Knife and it has magic powers,' said Zartak, holding the knife close to his daughter's face. He continued, 'It has belonged to the Zartak family for generations. Your great grandfather, Zoltan, came by it after a bitter feud with the Ongar family, who had abducted a Zartak child.'

'What does the writing on the blade of the knife say?' asked Rosa, who could read Hungarian although she was unfamiliar with Gothic letters at the time.

Zartak leant over the fire and held the knife close to his face to enable him to read the minute letters. He started to read aloud:

'If the Zartak Knife is taken by force from a Zartak hand, Zartak shall cease to live and his first-born child shall live in torment and die in ruin.'

Zartak turned the knife over to enable him to read the writing on the other side of the blade.

'But if the first-born child of the first-born child regains the knife, that child will experience everlasting fame, riches and joy.

Zartak took some folded parchment with cramped writing on it from an oblong wooden box and showed it to Rosa. The words 'The Legend of Zartak' were engraved on a plaque on the outside of the box in tiny Gothic letters.

'If I come to any harm,' said Zartak, 'look after the box and the parchment inside it and don't lose them. You're to give the box to your first-born child.'

'What does the writing on the parchment in the box say?' asked Rosa.

'It describes in greater detail the Legend of the Zartak Knife and the slaying of the Ongars who sought to destroy the House of Zartak.'

'What do you mean? We've never lived in a house,' said Rosa.

'A house does not necessarily mean a building with four walls and a roof. It means brethren. Zartaks don't die in their beds. They live and die by the weapons of their tradition.'

Dawn broke after a bitterly cold night. Night had turned to day and then to late afternoon. Zartak and Rosa clung to each other once more in a vain attempt to protect themselves from the cold. Zartak got out of the caravan and lifted Rosa to the ground, having kissed her gently on the forehead. He was brooding and moody and she sensed his anxiety.

The Zartaks were on their way to the check-point about a hundred yards ahead, manned by four sinister-looking Russian guards. It was then about four-thirty in the afternoon.

'Are those men dangerous?' Rosa asked, her voice raised, pointing to the guards.

'For mercy's sake, keep your voice down,' whispered Zartak, adding, 'they are unlikely to be dangerous unless you disobey me. Here's the box with the parchment rolled up inside it. Keep it and if anything happens to me pass it on to your first-born child, as I told you before. I'm going to give one of the men the passports,' he added.

'He will probably accept them. If he doesn't, crawl under the barrier while I talk to him, and run as far and as fast as you can. Whatever you do, don't stop running and don't turn round. Also, don't drop the box that I've given you. Guard it with your life. I'll catch up with you but don't hang about waiting for me.'

Rosa began to cry. Rogue, ruffian, murderer, thief and liar though he may have been, Zartak was a loving and indulgent parent and she was terrified of losing him.

The father and daughter reached the frontier where there were four guards. They were all young and they carried rifles with bayonets attached to them. They were wearing Russian Army jackets.

'Your papers,' said one of the guards peremptorily.

Zartak smiled and handed the two passports to the guard who found them suspicious.

'I'm not satisfied that your passports are in order. Wait here.'

Zartak lost his head. As he reached for the Zartak Knife, the guard hit him on the head with his rifle butt. Zartak struggled to get to his feet and pulled out the knife. Another guard shot him in the chest, just missing his heart, and the knife fell from his hand. Rosa had already crawled under the barrier, clutching the box containing the parchment.

Zartak tried desperately to get her attention.

'Keep running and don't turn round!' His voice was scarcely above a croak and Rosa couldn't hear his words, only the sound of his voice.

The guard then shot Zartak in the head, killing him instantly. Rosa had never heard guns before and she had no idea that they were harmful. She saw her father lying on the ground but assumed that he would overpower the guards with the Zartak Knife.

Once on Austrian soil, Rosa went on running for about three quarters of a mile until she felt that her lungs were crammed with ice.

She collapsed, still clutching the box which Zartak had given her. She was exhausted. Two hours passed. Night had fallen. She still believed that her father would come and find her, and fell asleep in the frozen undergrowth, having assumed she would wake up in Zartak's arms.

When she woke up several hours later, she found herself in bed in a room with a large crucifix on a wall whose ceiling was supported by gaunt-looking Gothic arches. Her chest ached and she had a fever. She was in a convent. She had managed to hold onto the box which her father had given her. A log fire burned in the grate and three nuns stood by her bedside. Sister Brigitta was the friendliest of the three and was the only one who spoke Hungarian.

'A hiker found you in the dense wood some three quarters of a mile away from the Austrian border. You were lucky not to have been devoured by wolves. You must try to get what rest you can. You're not very well. You've got a fever. We are going to look after you for the time being,' said Brigitta kindly.

'I want my father,' said Rosa urgently.

'Perhaps we can try to find him for you. When did you last see him?'

Rosa told Brigitta her story. Brigitta laid her hands on her head and kissed her on the cheek without being able to give her any information about her father.

'Do you want me to look after the box which you've got with you?' asked Brigitta kindly.

'No, my father gave it to me and he said I can't part with it.'

'That's all right, my child,' said Brigitta who was intrigued rather than nosy.

Apart from Brigitta, the other nuns spoke to Rosa in German. She was an expert linguist and after a short time, her German became as good as her Hungarian. Outwardly, she appeared to mourn her father less and less. By talking about him to Brigitta, she managed to exorcise, if only superficially, the pain that she suffered on his account.

* * *

Four months passed. It was a hot June day. Rosa woke up one morning and found Brigitta standing by her bedside, smiling.

'I've got some good news for you,' said the sympathetic nun.

Rosa smiled for the first time since her stay in the convent.

'Have you found my father?' she asked assertively.

'No, but a kind English lady is calling on us today. She is going to be your new mother. Her name is Miss Jeanette

23

Cavendish. She speaks fluent German, so you'll be able to understand what she says.'

* * *

Jeanette Cavendish was a fifty-one-year-old Presbyterian Scot, who worked for an agency specializing in the adoption of Hungarian refugee children. She had a sister called Geraldine, with whom she did not get on, and had no other siblings. Her mother, still living, was called Jean and Jeanette did not get on with her either. As Jeanette had never had a way with men, she had remained a virgin and a spinster but she had longed to bring up an abandoned waif. She had never felt genuine tenderness or compassion for children but the idea of bringing up a child gave her a sense of self-righteous pleasure.

Jeanette was the daughter of a millionaire called Jack Cavendish, with whom she got on well and who had made his money in property development. After her father's death, Jeanette inherited a large house in Belgravia (in London), a farm at least five thousand acres in size near Aylesbury in Buckinghamshire, an E-Type Jaguar, several horses and a pony. Near the house was a tennis court and a swimming pool, also owned by Jeanette. Geraldine, her sister, inherited a sizeable part of her father's fortune as well.

Apart from the advantage of being seen to be charitable, Jeanette sought companionship in old age and was prepared to suffer the inconvenience of bringing up a child to this end.

She was a tall woman and was elegant rather than pretty.

She had light brown hair, with blonde streaks, brown eyes and a pointed nose. She was wearing a Harris tweed cape over a neat beige cotton dress and a deerstalker's cap. Despite her cotton dress, she was overdressed for the time of year. When she arrived at the convent, Rosa was also wearing a cotton dress which Brigitta had made for her. Brigitta eased her forward to shake hands with Jeanette who addressed her in German. Jeanette was nervous and her manner was stiff, awkward and unwelcoming. Rosa continued to clutch the box which Zartak had given her.

'I'm going to give you a new home. We're going to England,' Jeanette forced herself to say stiffly, adding the words, 'I'm very rich,' which she regretted and genteelly cleared her throat.

'I don't want to go to England,' said Rosa defiantly. 'I don't speak English and I want my father.'

'Your father was killed at the frontier dividing Hungary from Austria. He was trying to escape from Hungary to Austria. In England, you will learn English. I have organized a governess for you. Once you have mastered the language, you will go to an English school. Are you fond of animals?'

'Horses, yes. My father and I had a cart horse which towed our caravan, and another cart horse before that but it died.'

'I live on a farm, said Jeanette, adding, 'you will have plenty of contact with horses.'

'I don't mind having contact with horses but I don't want any contact with *you*,' said Rosa rudely.

25

Rosa backed away from Jeanette and put her right arm round Brigitta's waist. She clutched the box which her father had given her under her left arm and sucked her thumb.

'You won't have much of a time if you stay here all your life,' said Brigitta guardedly, adding, 'I think you will be very happy once you have settled in England.'

There followed a distressing and harrowing scene. Rosa clung to Brigitta's robes as well as the box. Then she let out a strange, unearthly, mournful wail which continued for about five minutes. While Jeanette's E-Type Jaguar, with all the windows open, pulled away and Brigitta waved from the doorway of the convent where Rosa had been staying, the nun was unable to tell the difference between the child's inconsolable moans of grief and the howling of the wolves in the dense wood.

* * *

Hillyfields Farm, near Aylesbury in Buckinghamshire, was an extremely grand property, surrounded by pretty, undulating countryside. In the drawing-room was a grand piano. Rosa had never seen one before but she noticed that it had the same keyboard as her father's accordion. Her father had taught her to play some Hungarian folk songs which she was able to play without music sheets, working out the left hand notes as if she had been taught.

'What is in that box which you are clinging to, Rosa?' asked Jeanette, her tone unfriendly and interfering.

'It's a box which my father gave me. I've got to keep it

with me, he said, and pass it on to my first-born child,' replied Rosa aggressively.

'Very well. I suppose you can keep it,' said Jeanette, reluctantly, adding, 'I'm at a loss to understand where you get your musicianship from, but I don't see why you shouldn't have proper piano lessons.'

At eight o'clock every morning, a governess came to Jeanette's house to teach Rosa English, Latin, French, history, geography and arithmetic. There followed a break of about twenty minutes, during which Rosa had a glass of milk and some chocolate biscuits. A piano teacher took over at eleven o'clock to teach the waif until one-thirty. At lunch every day, Jeanette sat in silence with Rosa. Jeanette was too stiff and awkward to enable any form of conversation to flow freely and Rosa was too insolent and rebellious to respond to what few words she uttered. In the afternoons, at her own request, Rosa wandered round the farm and helped in the stables. This was something which she really enjoyed doing.

* * *

By the time she had been on the farm for five years, she was ten years old and spoke English like a native.

'I think it's time you and I had a little talk,' Jeanette said to her one sunny summer's morning at breakfast (in English).

'If it is, it's about the first time you've spoken to me since you brought me here.'

Jeanette let this ride.

'Your English is very good and you haven't got a trace

of a foreign accent. However, Rosa is not an English name. Now that you are living in England, you will answer to the name of Jessie. I think that's a very nice name. Henceforth, your surname will be Cavendish, like mine, and not Zartak.'

'Rosa Zartak is the only name I'll answer to. Rosa is the name my father chose for me and my surname has always been Zartak.'

'Your father is dead and any impertinence from you will be punished.'

'There's no proof that he's dead.'

'There is. He was shot at the Austrian frontier.'

'Rosa is still my name and I won't answer to the name of Jessie,' repeated the ten-year-old girl, obstinately.

Jeanette was about to slap Jessie but the child hurriedly got down from the table, brushed past her foster mother and rushed out into the yard. Digby Taylor, a fifteen-year-old groom, was saddling one of Jeanette's horses. He had a kindly and attractive face and thick, jet-black hair, like Jessie's and her father's.

'Hullo. You must be Miss Jessie Cavendish. My name's Digby Taylor.' His voice was hoarse and he had a strong Buckinghamshire accent. Jessie began to cry. Digby's friendliness brought Jeanette's permanent coldness to the surface. Also, the colour of his hair reminded her of her father.

'I'll show you something that will cheer you up,' said Digby, 'Jo-jo's just had a foal. Let's go and see Jo-jo and her foal.'

Digby produced an apple from his pocket for Jo-jo. He

28

didn't give one to the foal as the foal was not old enough to eat one.

'Have you been working on the farm for long?' asked Jessie.

'I was born on the farm. My father's Miss Cavendish's gardener, I am her groom, and my mother cleans her house. You've got a beautiful cat-like face. I'm going to address you as "Cat Face", if I may.'

'I don't mind,' said Jessie. 'Cat Face is a much nicer name than "Jessie" which my foster mother makes me answer to. My original name was Rosa, Rosa Zartak to be precise.'

Digby showed Jessie round the farm and it started to rain. He took her to a small outhouse where he lived with his parents, known as the lodge.

'My father's never here in the afternoon and my mother's upstairs resting. I'll make toast and honey by the fire. If you like, I'll take you riding tomorrow on the pony Miss Cavendish has bought for you. Have you ridden before?'

Jessie was touched by Digby's friendliness towards her and was reminded of her father once more.

'No. I've only been accustomed to travelling in a caravan pulled by a cart horse,' she said, adding, 'my father used to own the caravan. We had two cart horses. One of them died.'

'How old are you?'

'Ten.'

'I'll take you on the leading rein if you like. How about tomorrow afternoon?'

'Anything to get away from her.'

'From whom?'

'My foster mother.'

'Why? Don't you like her?'

'She's not my real mother. One day, my father will find out where I am and he'll come and take me away from here,' said Jessie, not believing her own words.

Digby scratched the back of his head.

'But I thought your father was shot dead, begging your pardon, Cat Face.'

Jessie told Digby the Legend of the Zartak Knife. She also told him that she thought that her father had failed to catch up with her because he couldn't find her in the dense wood.

Digby didn't believe her but he admired her vivid imagination and was too kind-hearted to say that he thought that she was making it all up.

He took her riding on the Cavendish estate the next day. It was late July and the weather was unbearably hot. Jessie and Digby were wearing straw hats to protect themselves from the scorching sun. They came to a cornfield where they dismounted and sat on the ground.

'I've got an idea. Would you like me to show you how to make yourself sick, Cat Face? Then you can be sick in front of Miss Cavendish and shock her,' ventured Digby in a mischievous tone of voice.

Jessie watched him, fascinated.

'You pick one of these ears of corn and put it down your throat.'

Digby did a demonstration and was sick.

'I'll tell you a joke,' he said, after recovering his breath. 'There were these two ancient Romans, lying side by side on couches, stuffing their faces. One of them put a feather down his throat between courses and was sick over his friend who turned to him and shouted, "Oh, damn te!"'

Jessie laughed. Her shrill neighing laugh, starting on a high note and gradually going down the scale, was the most infectious laugh Digby had ever heard.

Jessie and Digby continued to see each other in the afternoons and by the time three years had passed they had become inseparable friends. Jessie had recently had her thirteenth birthday. Digby was dependent on Jessie because of her unusual laugh and seeming innocence. Jeanette allowed her to keep the box which her father had given her in the safe.

Jessie had found a proper replacement for her father and her walks and rides with Digby cheered her otherwise miserable existence. She began to write music and by the time she had been accepted by Waltham Abbey at the age of thirteen, she had already written two symphonies, both of which had been played on Radio Three under her original name. They were also available on long-playing records.

Jessie was precocious and advanced for her thirteen years and her relationship with Digby had become physical. They often had sex in a barn about half a mile away from the lodge. It was in the lodge that Digby regularly made toast and honey.

Meals with Jeanette continued in silence. Jessie's jet-black hair had grown down to her waist. This was the case even when she was a little girl. She was showing signs of coarseness and boorishness and her foster mother often flinched with shock on hearing her thick Buckinghamshire accent which she had picked up from Digby.

'The first thing that Waltham Abbey is going to teach you is to shed your horrible rustic accent. God knows, I'll be paying them enough,' said Jeanette unpleasantly, adding, 'I'm taking you there at the beginning of the autumn term. That will be this coming autumn.'

Jessie didn't answer and slouched over the table, deliberately holding her knife like a pencil as she shovelled cottage pie and carrots into her mouth.

'I also hope you'll be taught not to hold your knife like a farm hand.'

'I've had more love and kindness from what you call a farm hand than you would be capable of giving anyone in a lifetime,' said Jessie, her voice raised.

Jeanette got up and closed the door so that the butler and the cook wouldn't hear her. Rage often made her close to tears.

'If it hadn't been for my kindness, you would still have been wandering round wastelands with criminals and thieves, like the one you lived with in Hungary.'

'Calling my father a criminal and a thief now, are you, you old bitch?'

Jeanette took off her belt and struck Jessie across the face with it. Strangely, Jessie showed no outward sign of humiliation or pain. Jeanette regretted her action and behaved as if nothing had happened.

'Have you ever asked yourself just how much you begrudge my charity?'

'Charity? Charity? You call your treatment of me charity? You only adopted me so that other people would think what a kind woman you are. There's never been any kindness, pity or charity in you. You took me on to gratify your own vanity!' shouted Jessie.

'I'm not even going to give you the benefit of an audience to hear the poison drip from your fangs. I'm going to my room. Please be ready to leave in half an hour,' said Jeanette, her voice lowered and trembling with rage.

Jeanette realized that her foster daughter would never be a companion to her in old age. She bitterly regretted having adopted her and was relieved because her school would be taking her off her hands, if only temporarily.

Jessie failed to wipe the blood off her face. She changed into her school uniform, consisting of a navy blue tunic, a matching blazer, a blue and white pinstripe shirt and the royal blue Churchill House tie. As she pulled on her clothes, she struggled in vain to fight the tears that were shed, not because Jeanette had hit her, but because she couldn't bear to leave Digby. She loved the name Cat Face. She even preferred it to Rosa. Jeanette drove Jessie to Waltham Abbey School in her E-Type Jaguar and left her in the corridor while she spoke to Miss Armstrong, Jessie's housemistress, in her study.

'Jessie is by no means an easy child, I fear. You do not have an enviable task ahead of you. Her manners are dreadful. She is already sexually precocious and I have every reason to believe that she has been having carnal relations with my groom.'

33

Some of the sherry fell from Miss Armstrong's glass. (She was an extremely heavy drinker, particularly of sherry.)

'Heigh-ho, I have never had any difficulties in disciplining recalcitrant children,' she muttered.

While the two women were talking, Jessie wandered round the building until she found the music block, an entire corridor containing pianos in small cubicles. She heard the monotonous sound of girls playing up and down scales. As she entered one of the cubicles, she saw a frumpish girl with frizzy gingery hair, several years her senior, trying to play *Für Elise* which she did amazingly badly.

'If you can't play *Für Elise* better than that, you shouldn't bother to play it at all,' said Jessie rudely.

'Who are you when you're at home, you black-haired git?'

'Jessie Cavendish. My real name is Rosa Zartak but my foster mother has forced me to answer to the name of Jessie Cavendish. If I really like someone, I like them to address me as Cat Face. That excludes you.'

'There's blood running down the side of your face. How did it get there?'

Jessie was a hardened and habitual liar, like her father.

'My foster mother lashed me across the face with a cat o' nine tails because I passed her the pepper when she had asked me for the salt. Who are you?' she replied.

'My name is Janet Spencer and I'm a prefect. If you think I play this piece so badly, perhaps you'd care to show me how you think it *should* be played.'

Jessie went over to the piano, snatched the music sheet from the piano rack and threw it on to the floor. 'Someone like me wouldn't need this,' she said arrogantly. She played *Für Elise* animatedly and professionally, including the more complex part in the middle while Janet stared at her aghast. When she had finished, she picked up the music sheet and handed it to Janet, smiling mockingly.

'I don't blame your foster mother for lashing you across the face with a cat o' nine tails,' said the older girl.

'If you're as useless a prefect as you are a musician, all I can say is, God help you.'

'Get out of here, you little brat!'

* * *

For the first three weeks of the autumn term, Jessie worked hard at her music but neglected her studies. Her energy was intensified by the knowledge that she would soon be reunited with her beloved Digby on her first weekend out of school in three weeks' time. She had been sleeping on alternate nights and writing music on the nights that she stayed awake. She had already written four songs in a traditional Hungarian mode which were to be played in the school concert at the end of the autumn term.

It was a Saturday when Jeanette came to collect Jessie from her school. The time was twelve o'clock. When she got home, she scrambled out of Jeanette's E-Type Jaguar and rushed to the lodge, leaving the passenger's door open, to find Digby.

She saw a fire burning through the window of the lodge

and noticed the familiar smell of toast and honey. She went straight in.

'Digby, they're going to play my Hungarian songs in the school concert!' she shouted.

Digby was nowhere to be found in the lodge, so Jessie looked for him in the barn where the two had often rolled in the hay, when his father was working a fair distance away.

It was a damp October day and the hay in the barn was soft and mellow-scented. Instead of the comforting aura of warmth and safety which Jessie had previously associated with the barn, there was a stifling and overpowering atmosphere of stillness and foreboding. She could not understand what it was that frightened her but she knew that she would soon find Digby and overcome her fear. She climbed over the mounted-up bales of hay and went to the other side of the barn, expecting to find him there. When she found him, he had his back to her.

'Digby, I've got some wonderful news about my Hungarian songs!' she shouted.

Digby didn't answer. She went over and stood in front of him. His eyes were vacant and protruded from their sockets. His face was ashen and his lips were blue. A rat was eating its way through one of his shoes. His feet were touching the floor of the barn. Jessie moved closer and found a tightened piece of rope round his neck. Digby had hanged himself from a beam. Jessie's immediate reaction was to run away from the scene in order to undo what had happened by ignoring it.

She returned to the lodge, telling herself that she hadn't

seen what she had seen and assumed that Digby would be waiting to make her toast and honey. Through the window of the lodge she saw a bare arm holding a fork with a piece of bread at the end of it in front of the fire. She thought that everything was all right and went straight in.

'I'm so relieved you're here, Digby,' she said, adding, 'I've just seen something horrible in the barn. There was a life-like statue of you hanging from a beam. If you put it there, I don't think that's very funny.'

The person making the toast turned round and rose to his feet. He was shorter than Digby and had curly, blond hair covered by a leather cap.

'Good morning to you, Miss Jessie. Teddy's my name, Teddy Armitage. I'm Miss Cavendish's groom and my father, Gerry Armitage, is her gardener. My mother is Grace Armitage, her cleaner.' He spoke with a Buckinghamshire accent like Digby's.

Jessie was terrified.

'I don't understand. Where are Digby and his parents?'

'I've got some very sad news,' said Teddy. 'Your foster mother turned them all off her land, Miss Jessie. She found out about Digby and you and she said that things weren't proper between you. Digby's father couldn't get a job anywhere in the county. Nor could his wife. In the end, they both found work in London and Digby was told to go with them.'

'What happened to Digby?' asked Jessie. This time, she was hysterical.

Teddy cleared his throat and shuffled from one foot to the other.

'He wouldn't get off Miss Cavendish's land, Miss Jessie. He had a broken heart. He said he was going to wait till you came home so that he could say goodbye to you properly. He thought you would be home first thing this morning, so he went to the barn and waited. When you didn't come, I think he must have gone off his head. Whatever you do, don't go into the barn,' said Teddy.

Jessie clutched Teddy's arm and started screaming.

'Digby's dead, isn't he?'

A silence ensued. Teddy lowered his head and removed his cap. His voice was scarcely above a whisper.

'Yes, Miss Jessie. He was hurt so bad that he hanged himself but he left this letter which he asked me to give to you.'

Teddy made Jessie some tea which calmed her a little. Digby's letter was written in a backward-slanting copperplate hand. His written English was remarkably correct and devoid of grammatical errors. It was grossly at variance with his strong Buckinghamshire accent.

The letter said:

My beloved Cat Face,
We were never meant for happiness, you and I, you beautiful, raven-tressed gypsy girl, with your lovely cat-like face. You once told me the Legend of the Zartak Knife which says that your father's first-born child will live in torment and die in ruin. If you hadn't told me that, there might have been some hope and we could have run away together. You are cursed

38

by a wicked hand and I cannot save you from Fate. But we will meet again, dear Cat Face, in a better life than this. Your ever-loving Digby.

* * *

Whatever Jeanette had taken away from Jessie, she couldn't take away the letter declaring Digby's love for her. She hid it in the sole of one of her shoes, which Teddy nailed back on for her.

'You've been ever so good to me, Teddy. I'd like to think we were friends,' said Jessie, adding, 'people I like call me Cat Face. It's my nickname. I'd like you to call me that as well. It was Digby who first called me by that name.'

'I'll be your friend, Cat Face. I think that woman's nasty and cruel. You need a bit of kindness. I'm on your side if no one else is.'

Teddy's friendly words gave Jessie courage and enabled her to face another lunch with Jeanette.

'You haven't spent the first part of your weekend out with me. I don't see much point in taking you out from school in future. But at least you've managed to shed that common Buckinghamshire accent,' said Jeanette.

Jessie threw a plate at Jeanette and shrieked at the top of her voice.

'How dare you think that I owe any of my time to you! Why the hell should I? You're no more than a common murderer!'

'So you're prepared to call me a murderer, are you?'

39

Jessie lurched across the table and pointed her fork at Jeanette.

'I'm calling you a murderer because you *are* a murderer. Your hands are bloodier than Lady Macbeth's. It was you who killed my Digby.'

'I sometimes wonder if you would be better off in a mental institution, Jessie. Digby was a base, low-bred ruffian who interfered with you when you were under age. I turned him and his parents off our land because he was, and probably still is, an adulterous, oafish lout.'

Jessie walked round to Jeanette's side of the table. 'I think if I stayed in this room a moment longer, I'd kill you. I'm going to my room until tomorrow when it's time for me to go back to school,' she shouted at the top of her voice, adding, 'one of the many reasons I'm keeping away from you and refraining from hitting you is that I should imagine borstal food tastes even worse than the muck I get in this house!'

Jeanette grabbed her foster daughter as she rushed towards the door. She dragged her to the dining table and pushed her face downwards on the table while plates and glasses fell to the floor. She removed Jessie's briefs and thrashed her repeatedly on the bottom with the buckle end of her belt.

'You'll hear from the NSPCC about this, you filthy old sadist!' screamed Jessie.

'And you'll hear from Miss Armstrong about your abuse of my goodwill. Not only that, I'd like you to get your hair cut. It doesn't suit you that long.'

40

'In no way am I having my hair cut. My father liked it to reach my waist and so do I,' said the girl.

Marples, the butler, came into the room to clear the table but when he saw what was going on, he coughed sheepishly and withdrew, walking backwards with his head bowed, as if in the presence of royalty.

'You've never shown goodwill to anyone but yourself,' said Jessie quietly.

Jeanette took her earrings off and put them back on again which she always did when she was tense.

'I'm going to discuss with Miss Armstrong the possibility of your seeing a psychiatrist,' she said, her voice raised.

* * *

Marcia found Jessie sitting on a windowsill outside the house study on Sunday evening. It was very windy and the window was wide open. She was crying. Jessie's tears were hot and silent and seemed to Marcia to be caused by some innermost torture deep within her soul. Her long, jet-black hair was blowing in the wind like a flag of death.

'What's the matter, Cat Face?' asked Marcia.

Jessie didn't answer straight away and turned her back on Marcia.

'You can tell me. I won't tell anyone.'

'Do your remember me telling you about Digby Taylor?'

'Of course I do. What's happened? Has he gone off with someone else?'

'He's dead. My foster mother had him and his parents turned off her land. He's hanged himself.'

The shock didn't register with Marcia straight away.
'I can't do very much to help you but there is one thing I can do.'
'What?'
'I can share my Bounty bar with you,' said Marcia kindly.

* * *

The head of house, Hilda Swain, sat at the head of one of the tables in the dining room that evening with Marcia and Jessie sitting on either side of her. Hilda turned to Marcia.

'When you're sitting next to a prefect during a meal, you don't sit in silence. You make intelligent conversation. You've got one minute in which to speak,' she said in a bullying tone of voice.

'I can't speak to rote and I've got nothing to say,' replied Marcia rudely.

'I'm afraid that's not good enough. You are at this school to learn good manners which encompasses the art of making polite conversation at meals.'

'I am already late handing in my history essay and that's worrying me so much that I don't feel like talking to anyone. You'll have to accept that,' said Marcia.

Hilda had short, greasy blonde hair with tight natural curls and piercing blue eyes which had pupils like pin heads. Her voice was shrill and her intonation sharp and biting. She was seventeen years old.

'I am not prepared to accept that at all. Your history essay is not of any interest, either to me or anyone else at this table,' said the older girl in a cutting tone of voice.

'What's your history essay about?' asked Jessie.

'Henry the Second and his quarrel with Thomas à Becket.'

Hilda noticed that Jessie's eyes were inflamed. A surge of protective pity suddenly broke down her viciousness.

'We rather exhausted the subject of Henry the Second's quarrel with Thomas à Becket at lunch, don't you think, Marcia? As your conversational ability appears to be so limited, I will seek out the other young lady as a more stimulating companion.'

She turned to Jessie.

'What's your name?' she asked.

'Well, my real name is Jessie but people I like call me Cat Face.'

'Tell me about yourself, Cat Face. Is it true you are a musician?' asked Hilda in a friendly tone of voice.

Jessie fixed Hilda with a surly stare. Hilda mistook her arrogant insolence for sadness.

'I can't tell you anything about myself because I don't know anything about myself, except that I play the piano, the harp and the guitar and I write music.'

'You must be a genius, Cat Face! I can't say I know much about music so you'll have to enlighten me. All I know are the treble notes. How does it go, All Fat Boys Eat Grass, isn't it?' said Hilda in a genial tone of voice.

Jessie laughed in a good-natured way. She had suddenly begun to like Hilda.

'I think you mean, Every Good Boy Deserves Fruit.'

43

'I can hardly see Marcia, who finds it so hard to string a sentence together, writing music. By the way, I like your beautiful, waist-length, jet-black hair. It really suits you. It goes with your pretty grey eyes and your cat-like face.'

Jessie recognized Hilda to be a bully, but she saw in her a maternal instinct which she craved. She went out of her way to flatter her.

'I very much regretted not being able to see you as Hamlet last term. I hear you were wonderful,' she said sycophantically.

Hilda patted her on the shoulder while Marcia scowled at her.

'What a charming thing to say!' exclaimed Hilda, adding, 'Of course, my performance would have been brilliant if I hadn't had a headache. However, I think I was quite reasonable. What did you think of my performance, Marcia, or were you so engrossed in thinking about yourself that you were unaware of what was going on?'

'Laurence Olivier* is by far the best Hamlet I've ever seen,' said Marcia cheekily. She continued, 'You could have done well to have taken a few tips from him. If you want my candid opinion, your *To Be or Not to Be* speech was a gas. You sounded like a recalcitrant debutante giving instructions to her hairdresser.'

The other girls at the table sniggered into their hands.

'You insolent little bitch! I can tell by looking at you that you're never going to be attractive to the opposite sex,' said Hilda.

*A famous English actor, now deceased.

'That's interesting. Why don't you ask my boyfriend whether or not I'm attractive to the opposite sex? Besides, he has often said how much he likes my plaited red hair.'

'Next time, don't give an opinion until you're asked for one,' said Hilda.

'I *was* asked. It was you who asked me. You must have a very short memory,' said Marcia, adding, 'I'm surprised you were able to remember your lines.'

Miss Armstrong rang the bell. The girls stood up and Hilda said a Grace in Latin, her voice trembling with rage. The girls filed out of the room. Hilda took Marcia aside.

'I could make your life fucking vile if I wanted to,' she said.

'I have been brought up not to use obscene words, but if you are going to make my life what you said you'd make it, you will have my father to reckon with. He is the Editor-in-Chief of two prominent newspapers.'

'My father's infinitely more important than yours, you little cow. You will learn *To Be or Not to Be* by heart and recite it to me in the prefects' study tomorrow morning before breakfast.' (Hilda's father was the Tory MP for South Wiltshire. He did not have any other duties.)

'What if I don't?' asked Marcia.

'You will be given *O, That This Too Too Sullied Flesh Would Melt* to learn as well.'

Marcia reluctantly learnt the words of *To Be or Not to Be* by heart and recited them to Hilda in the prefects' study the following morning. Her task was not difficult. She had a photographic memory and the words were easy for her to memorize.

* * *

Later that week, Marcia found Jessie in the house study, making a miniature cardboard stage, surrounded by an ornate theatre, its seats and boxes lined with dark red velvet. The floor of the stage was covered with minute writing. Marcia picked up the miniature theatre and held it close to her face. She was just able to read the writing, without straining her eyes.

My feet they are sore and my limbs they are weary,
Long is the way and the mountains are wild.
Soon will the twilight close moonless and dreary,
Over the path of the poor orphan child.

'I made those words up last night. Do you like them?' asked Jessie.

'You're a bloody liar, Cat Face!' exclaimed Marcia. 'You know perfectly well that those are the words of Charlotte Brontë. The poem comes from *Jane Eyre*, which you said was your favourite book. You must have taken some time making that thing. What's it all in aid of?'

'It's Hilda's birthday tomorrow and I've made this as a present for her. She's like a mother to me. She looks just like my vision of the great god Pan, except that she's a girl.'

Marcia was immediately reminded of Elizabeth Barrett

Browning's poem, entitled *A Musical Instrument*. The words of the poem were hard for her to understand and started off with the question, *What was he doing, the great god Pan, Down in the reeds by the river?*

'*The great god Pan?*'* These words were meant to be poetic, but to Marcia they were nauseating.

Marcia returned to the matter in hand.

'You must be raving mad, going out of your way for that odious old bag.'

For the first time that she had known Jessie, Marcia saw on her friend's face a peculiar expression of reverence. Jessie laid the miniature theatre gently on the table.

'Only the best is good enough for Hilda, who is like a goddess,' she said, her voice lowered, as if she were praying.

The bell rang. It was time for the girls to leave the building to get ready for the first chapel service of the day. Marcia saw Jessie hurrying upstairs.

'Come on, Cat Face! Where are you going?'

'I've got to get Hilda's clothes ready for the laundry.'

'This isn't a boys' school. Girls don't have to fag. Did Hilda tell you you were to do these things for her?'

'She doesn't need to tell me. I look after her clothes because I love her.'

Marcia lost patience with Jessie.

'I don't understand why you waste so much time running round after Hilda,' she said, not without a twinge of jealousy.

---

*The author's parents had made her learn the first three verses of this poem, when they were told that she had broken windows in Ian Fleming's house at the age of eight. She only broke a couple of windows so she had no idea, at the time, what all the fuss was about.

'I wouldn't expect you to understand. You don't know what it's like not to have parents. You've got parents and siblings. All I've got is a foster mother who is cruel to me and whom I hate. I need someone to look up to.'

'You've still got Teddy Armitage. You said that he'd replaced Digby Taylor in your affections, didn't you?'

Hilda suddenly appeared from round the corner.

'What do you think you're doing? The bell rang ten minutes ago,' she said to Marcia.

'I'm waiting for Cat Face. She's gone upstairs to get your clothes ready for the laundry.'

Jessie came down five minutes later.

'I've sorted out your clothes, Hilda, and I've changed your sheets as well.'

'You're a wonderful girl, Cat Face. You're my friend for life. Do you think you could lend me your make-up case as well? Brian's coming out from Eton for the weekend and we're seeing each other on Saturday.'

'Yes, certainly, Hilda. If you give me your dress on Friday evening, I will iron it for you.'

The eyes of the older and younger girl met. Hilda's expression was that of the spoiled adolescent who had never been thwarted. Jessie's was of the permanently thwarted waif who would never live to be spoiled.

To Marcia, the look they exchanged was one of mutual adoration. She mimicked Jessie's voice and accentuated her lisp.

'I've sorted your clothes out, Hilda. I'll iron your dress, Hilda. I'll leave you in each other's company. I think you're

48

both absolutely nauseating. Are you sleeping together?'

'I've had enough of your disgusting insolence, Marcia Ford,' said Hilda. 'You will learn *O, That This Too Too Sullied Flesh Would Melt* and recite it to me tomorrow morning in the prefects' study before breakfast.'

* * *

Three years passed. Hilda had gone to Oxford to read English. She was in the Dramatics Society at her college. She once played the part of Juliet. As she lay flat on her back, at the end of the play, an ambulance siren was heard outside the theatre. Instead of taking this as a joke, Hilda took it extremely seriously, and continued to lie on her back, shaking with rage.

Marcia and Jessie had just turned sixteen years old and were about to take their 'O' levels. Jessie had completed four symphonies and was working on an opera of *Jane Eyre*. Marcia and Jessie spent most of their time in the company of a few other girls: Julia Wentridge, whom Marcia had known since they were both about nine years old, Ruth Gould, Miranda Evans and Buffy Dwyer. Marcia and Julia had been at prep school together. They had passed their Common Entrance exam to determine whether or not they were bright enough to go to Waltham Abbey.

Julia tended to dominate the group. So did Ruth. An only child, Julia was a vivacious, glamorous brunette with shoulder-length curly dark brown hair, navy blue eyes that were never focused on one object for more than a second at a time, and a retrousse nose. She was devoted to her invalid father who had a serious heart complaint and who permanently hovered between life and death. He was the owner of a well-known cosmetics company called Wentridge Cosmetics, which was near Basingstoke in Hampshire.

Julia was mature for her sixteen years and was emotionally involved with two roguish, psychologically complex brothers called the Oppenheimers who were at Marlborough.*

Ruth Gould was a flashy redhead and was very clever. She was friendly with Julia, although both girls competed for the role of group leader. Ruth's father was a wealthy dentist with a thriving Harley Street practice, and a large house in Golders Green. She, too, was mature for her years and went out with a boy called Jacob Cohen who was the son of her father's best friend. Jacob was at Eton and Ruth planned to marry him after leaving school, followed by university. (She intended to read philosophy.)

Miranda, a parson's daughter, was the laughing stock of the group. She had long brown hair parted in the centre, and because she was plain, she covered as much of her face with it as she could. She had had little luck with the opposite sex, and as if to come to terms with her failure to attract young men, she considered sexual relations with them before marriage to be, in her own words, 'very regrettable'. It was Julia's and Ruth's pity alone which enabled her to join the group.

Buffy Dwyer was the group bitch. She came from a loud, *arriviste* family living in Hertfordshire. Her father had been a bus driver from Camberwell in south London but he
_____
*A public school for boys.

had won a fortune on the pools. In order to hide her guilt about her having come from rags to riches, without her father actually working to gain his wealth, Buffy worked as an air hostess for British Airways in later years. Sometimes she worked as a prostitute.

Buffy had a shock of thick, crudely bleached hair, a grotesquely round, melon-like face and a bevy of vibrating chins. Her speech was high-pitched and gabbled to hide her south London vowels. She bore a permanent grudge against children of established wealth and sneered at people with cultural interests – and in particular at people who wrote books. This, combined with an over-glamorized view of her own sex appeal, made her unpopular with other girls. Buffy's only attributes were her long slim legs and her beautiful artist's hands which she flaunted like a transvestite clubber whenever she spoke.

Julia and Ruth had taken Buffy on because they were intrigued by her aggressive vulgarity, and her habit of picking men up at bus-stops and on trains and receiving money from them in return for sexual favours.

Buffy remained the same later on in life. Jessie had seen her, by chance, working as an air hostess on a plane from Heathrow to Orly, before she (Jessie) was due to play the piano at La Salle Pleyel, a concert hall in Paris. She had been asked to play Rachmaninov's Second Piano Concerto in C minor.

Tadeuz Sikorsky, an ageing Polish war veteran with an artificial leg, was occupying a seat by the window of the plane. The Pole was in extreme discomfort but Buffy

51

wouldn't let him sit in the only available bulkhead seat, due to her bloody-mindedness.

'I've got a right to sit in a bulkhead seat,' the Pole wailed, adding, 'I deliberately got to the airport early so that I could book a bulkhead seat.'

'That's tough. The bulkhead seats are all occupied,' lied Buffy.

'Listen, young lady. I'm a Pole. I know that what you say isn't true. I lost my leg fighting during World War II for the freedom which young people like you now enjoy.'

Jessie stared at Buffy with loathing from across the aisle but Buffy ignored her.

'You seem to think that the Poles were the only bloody people who suffered during World War II,' said Buffy angrily.

Hot tears were rolling down Sikorsky's cheeks.

'Please young lady, you've got no idea how much pain I'm in.'

Suddenly, he unstrapped his artificial leg and laid it on the floor. Its foul-smelling, septic stump flapped up and down involuntarily and with hideous rapidity. The Pole appeared to ignore this and continued to stare at Buffy who peered at his amputated leg with disgust. Jessie became disturbed and agitated, called another air hostess and ordered a double gin and tonic.

The Pole opened his briefcase and pulled out a book entitled, *I Fought the Führer* by Tadeuz Sikorsky.

'Please, young lady, I would like you to have a copy of my book. If I may, I will sign it for you. Only, please, let me have a bulkhead seat. I know there's one available. I'm in so much pain.' Sikorsky began to weep uncontrollably.

When Buffy spoke, it was with extraordinary hatred and resentment because a writer had actually dared to offer her one of his books. She gabbled like a chipmunk and jerked her cheaply bleached head from side to side, flicking her quivering chins. Her words seemed to bounce out of her mouth as if they were propelled from an evil spring within.

'I don't want it, you old bastard!' she said, her voice raised. 'I don't want any book written by you 'cos I know what sort of a book it's gonna be!'

Jessie suddenly noticed Buffy's initialled Dior shoes which a punter had given her during her streetwalking days.

'What does C.D. stand for, Buffy – Carnival Doll?' she shouted.

* * *

The group of girls walked from Churchill House to the main school, talking about men and they walked back to Churchill House after lessons, talking about men. Once in the bootroom, they continued to talk about men. Jessie, Julia and Buffy sat in the basins. Marcia and Miranda sat on the floor and Ruth lay down on one of the benches underneath the coats.

'Is it true you're screwing your father's chauffeur's son, Marce? Are you going to marry him?' said Julia to Marcia.

'That would be a bit *déclassé*, don't you think? Who wants to talk about me? Cat Face has had more men than any of us put together.'

'Well, there's Teddy, my foster mother's groom,' Jessie began, 'but he's not anything like as good as the boy who comes over the fence by one of the lacrosse pitches. His name is Garry Winters. I think Marcia's father's chauffeur's the best. He's the most experienced because he's older. I've never tried his son, though.'

'You are quite incorrigible, Cat Face!' exclaimed Julia.

'Let's hear about Marcia's father's chauffeur, Cat Face,' said Ruth.

'He's wonderful. We go into the woods while we're waiting for Marcia to come out to her father's Bentley. He's pretty hot on fellatio.'*

'What's fellatio?' asked Miranda innocently.

'Of course, no one would expect someone with *your* lack of sexual experiences to know what fellatio is,' said Buffy bitchily, adding, 'besides, you haven't contributed much to this conversation. Perhaps you'd care to tell us about your own sexual experiences, or are you saving your virginity till after you've had plastic surgery?'

'You really are a proverbial bitch, Buffy!' shouted Ruth.

'I don't think so. If this were said to me, I'd take it on the chin.'

'Which chin, sister?' said Marcia, as disagreeably as possible.

All the girls laughed except for Buffy who left the bootroom in tears.

'I'm beginning to find all this talk about sex and men

---

* Oral sex

rather tedious. Let's talk about something else,' suggested Jessie, adding, 'I know a really hilarious joke: there were these two ancient Romans lying side by side on couches, stuffing their faces. One of them put a feather down his throat between courses, and was sick over his friend who turned to him and shouted, "Oh, damn te!"' Jessie gave her usual neighing laugh which gradually went down the scale.

'That's a bloody terrible joke, Cat Face!' exclaimed Marcia.

A silence ensued, which was broken by Julia. 'I dare say we can do without Buffy in future,' she said.

'You're right. I don't think my father would like her going round in the same group as me. My father's a good man and he doesn't like bitches,' said Ruth.

* * *

Julia invited Jessie to stay with her parents during the Easter holidays at the end of the spring term. The two girls were still sixteen years old. When Julia and her mother met Jessie at Basingstoke station, the rebel was extremely drunk. She was wearing dark glasses (although the sky was overcast), flared white trousers and a red sweater two sizes too big for her. She carried a guitar over her shoulder. Her feet were bare, her waist-length, jet-black tresses were loose and her feline face was covered with three layers of make-up.

The Wentridges lived in a seventeenth-century house near Basingstoke. Its interior was dark and austere with oak panelled walls everywhere. The oak dining-room table and tall upright chairs were seventeenth century like the rest of the house. The garden was several acres in size and consisted of freshly mown lawns, an empty swimming pool, which had just been painted, and a swing (for Julia).

When Julia, her mother and Jessie reached the house, Mr Wentridge was sitting in the drawing room, in a dressing gown, doing a jigsaw puzzle of a Hogarth painting, for Hogarth was his favourite painter.

Jessie, Julia and Mrs Wentridge entered the drawing room and Mr Wentridge leant across the table and extended his hand to Jessie in greeting.

'You'll have to excuse me for not being fully dressed and not getting up. I've been rather unwell of late,' he said apologetically.

Jessie was unaware of her host's illness and felt disappointed because he wasn't robust enough for her to flirt with him. She took his hand and gripped it very tightly until it hurt so much that he had to release it with his other hand. She eyed him lecherously.

'Pleased to meet you, Mr Wentridge!'

'I've heard all about you from Julia,' said Mr Wentridge, adding, 'I hear you're a musician. I believe they call you "Cat Face" at school. Do play something for me on the piano.' His voice was extremely frail due to his illness.

Jessie lurched over to the well-polished grand piano and played the first movement of Mozart's Sonata Number 11, without the score in the piano rack. She smiled lasciviously and stared at Mr Wentridge throughout her rendition. He clapped but even the exertion of clapping exhausted him. There was something about Jessie which he found uncanny and repellent. What turned him off her completely was the fact that she hadn't bathed for some time and smelled of stale sweat.

Suddenly, a gunshot was heard from the garden. Mrs Bambleberry, the parlour maid, rushed into the room, wringing her hands.

'It's them Oppenheimer brats, sir. They're in the empty swimming pool which has just been painted. One of them's shot the other in the leg. It's the thinner one who's been playing up as usual,' she said, adding, 'there's blood all over the place!'

Mr Wentridge sank deeply into his chair and clutched his throat.

'I don't care for either of those boys, Julia, or for your friend whom you call Cat Face,' he said, practically in a whisper, adding, 'I don't want any of them in the house again. Mark caused enough havoc in the neighbourhood when your other friend, Marcia, the maniac, came to stay when she was little more than a child. If you insist on seeing them all, you'll have to do so somewhere else.'

When Marcia, 'the maniac' had stayed with the Wentridge family during another school holiday (a summer holiday), six years before, aged ten, the Oppenheimers had stayed in the house as well. Mark had taken a shine to Marcia who was dressed in tight-fitting white jeans, and a tight white T-shirt. He had also taken a shine to her plaited red hair. Mark had dared Marcia to throw a brick at a passing sports car on the main road leading to London. Marcia never said 'no' to a dare and she had obliged, much to Mark's surprise but accompanying admiration. Later that day, when Marcia, Julia and the Oppenheimer boys had gone to the cinema, Mark had dared Marcia to go up to the fifty-year-old ice cream vendor and say, 'There's a very good-looking boy in the auditorium who'll fuck you for a shilling.'* Marcia had obliged again.

'There's a very good-looking boy in the auditorium who'll fuck you for a shilling,' Marcia had said to the ice cream vendor who had replied, in a heavy West Country brogue, 'Oh there is, is there? Tell the boy I'm worth a darned sight more than just one shilling.'

'Tell her she's only worth a shilling,' Mark had said. Marcia had repeated Mark's words to the ice cream vendor who had replied, 'Get out of 'ere and don't be so bloomin' cheeky.'

Eventually the police had been called and had asked Marcia what borstal she was from. She had been cautioned but not charged. She later told Jessie about her adventures while staying with Julia. Jessie was intrigued and amused. She greatly admired Marcia, who, she thought was afraid of nothing.

* * *

When Julia and Jessie were sixteen years old, the two girls were sitting on a dark brown velvet-covered sofa, waiting

---

*One shilling equals five pence.

to go out. Mrs Wentridge and her husband were already familiar with the shady reputation of the Oppenheimer brothers and with Marcia's delinquent behaviour. Mrs Wentridge offered Jessie a drink.

'Whisky, please.'

'Aren't you a little young?'

'I said – "whisky please".'

The older woman filled Jessie's glass with a modest amount of whisky but Jessie handed the glass back to her, with a snide expression on her face.

'Sorry. Did you want something in it?' asked Mrs Wentridge.

'Yes. More whisky,' replied Jessie rudely.

Mrs Wentridge was extremely irritated.

'I'm going to help your father up to bed. Please see that you are out of the house by the time I come down,' she said to her daughter, adding, 'the Cat Face girl is almost as badly behaved as your other friend, Marcia.'

* * *

The Oppenheimer brothers, who were both bearded, looked very alike. The only difference between them was that Jack was extremely stout whereas Mark was slimmer. Their facial expressions alternated between conspiratorial mischief and tormented despair. Both the brothers were later known for destructive jealousy and even violence towards women and both had a pathological dread of poverty.

Their paternal grandfather had served in India. While he was in India, his cook had fried his eggs in boot polish one morning, whereupon he had stormed into the kitchen and had slit the cook's throat.

Years later, he shot his wife dead during a dispute in which he accused her of having sex with other men, although he had had many affairs with other women. In other words, he was projecting his behaviour onto her. He shot her dead, and finally turned the gun on himself.

Jack, his grandson, was seventeen years old and was the elder of the Oppenheimer brothers. He was pink-cheeked and plump. Mark, aged sixteen, was paler than his brother, and had a disconcerting, nervous habit of pulling a flick-knife from his pocket and flicking it open and shut every time he was lost for words. Both brothers had haunted brown eyes. Mark's eyes were rather bloodshot and were even more haunted-looking than his brother's.

When Jessie and Julia met the brothers again in the bar of the Red Lion Hotel near Julia's parents' house, they looked hung over and worn out. The four of them ordered neat whisky. The two brothers parked their jaded eyes on Jessie. Her beatnik-like appearance, waist-length black hair and cat-like face appealed to them. Julia's appearance was more conservative than Jessie's. She was wearing an elegant dark red velvet trouser suit.

'I understand your father doesn't want us in the house,' said Jack to Julia.

'Since you two insist on walking about in the swimming pool when it's just been painted, shooting each other like a couple of cowboys in the Wild West, I hardly find that surprising. "There was blood all over the place," Mrs Bambleberry said.'

'What sort of gun was it, a twelve-bore shotgun?' asked Jessie, gazing lecherously at Mark.

'It was a Smith & Wesson, sexpot,' said Mark, smiling. He had a gold-plated lower front tooth which attracted Jessie.

A long silence ensued and Mark continued to flick his knife open and shut. The barman gave them all some neat whisky while Julia sat apart from the group, thinking about the Oppenheimer brothers. She was secretly in love with Mark because she had a perverse attraction towards unstable, violent young men, but she spent a lot of her time with Jack as an excuse to gain access to him. Jack intended to marry her and later did so when she became pregnant at the age of eighteen. The baby was conceived in the back of Jack's orange Ford Capri on the night of Marcia's eighteenth birthday party at the Savoy Hotel in London. Julia was prepared to go through the ceremony to ensure a continuation of her relationship with Mark. She once alarmed Mark by ringing him up and saying assertively, 'I want to have an unhealthy relationship with you.'

Mark had a shy streak and was by far the most melancholic and the darkest spirited of the two brothers. Julia was profoundly attracted to his despondency but was too frightened of his universally known destructiveness and viciousness towards women to spend any length of time with him.

It was not until later in life, long after Julia had divorced Jack, that Mark came to stay with her and her new husband, after his own marriage had failed as a result of his violent and unstable behaviour towards his wife. (He had inherited such behaviour from his grandfather.) Mark's and Julia's teenage attraction to each other was rekindled but Mark, who desperately wanted a reconciliation with his unwilling wife, overdosed himself in an obscure hotel and died.

Mark was powerfully attracted to Jessie.

'You're a musician, aren't you? Is it true that you play the guitar and the harp, as well as the piano?' he asked nervously.

'Why?' asked Jessie, her tone of voice inexplicably suspicious.

Mark felt ill at ease. He drank some more neat whisky and continued to play with his flick-knife.

'Do put that bloody thing away, Mark!' said Jack, but Mark ignored his elder brother and turned to Jessie once more.

'Why don't we go and eat? I'll do dinner tonight,' he said.

Jessie took a wad of twenty pound notes from her tattered, hippy handbag and waved the banknotes ostentatiously in front of the brothers. (She had stolen the money, which she had found in the waiting room at Waterloo Station.)

'I'm afraid I must contradict you. I'm taking *you* out but I'm only prepared to pay for you, Jack and myself. Why don't you go home, Julia? Your invalid father may need your help,' said Jessie in a bitchy tone of voice.

Julia was too shocked to show anger straight away and left without uttering a word. She took a taxi home. After dinner, Jessie had sex with Jack and Mark in turn in one of the Red Lion Hotel's lavatories. Julia's parents were asleep when Jessie returned to the house, accompanied by the Oppenheimers, even though they had all been banned from the house by Julia's father. Julia was in the living room, shaking with rage.

'I'll make it up to you, Jules,' said Jack.

Julia gave Jack a resounding slap on the ear.

'I'm surprised you dare show your faces in here. You know my father can't stand the sight of any of you,' she shouted.

The brothers followed Jessie upstairs. An expensive gold pill box was lying on Julia's bedside table with an engraving on it.

To dear Julia, with love from Mark.

Mark picked it up and handed it to Jessie.

'Please accept this gift to you for a lovely evening,' he said charmingly, adding, 'I love your pale, cat-like face and waist-length black tresses. You remind me of the poems of Edgar Allan Poe.'

Julia's mother turned Jessie out of the house the following morning, and she agreed to travel to London on the same train as the Oppenheimers. The train was bound for Waterloo Station and was one of the last of its kind to be divided into small compartments. Jessie sat between the Oppenheimer brothers and opposite them sat an elderly parson and a middle-aged man reading *The Guardian*.

The first movement of Mozart's Sonata Number 11 was ringing through Jessie's ears like tinnitus. She took Mark by the hand and led him to the lavatory. When they came back, she took Jack's hand and invited him out as well. After that, Mark dug his elder brother mockingly in the ribs and Jack blushed profusely on catching the parson's eye.

When Jessie had finished with Jack, she went out into the corridor and stood, looking out of the window. She was still wearing her flared white trousers which had become slightly soiled. She had on her sunglasses once more and was carrying her guitar over her shoulder. Her feet were bare as before. Mark joined her in the corridor. He gave her a shifty, sideways look and flicked his knife open and shut as he fought to find his words.

'What's Jack like, Cat Face?' he eventually ventured in a mischievous tone of voice.

Jessie gave her usual neighing laugh which went down the scale. Mark took her amusement to mean that his brother's performances had not been equal to his.

The Oppenheimer brothers politely waited for Jessie to get off the train and followed her. The parson laid his hands on her head as she walked off the train onto the platform.

'May God forgive you for your sins, my daughter,' he mumbled hoarsely.

Jessie jerked her head backwards and bared her teeth in a hideous grimace of defiance.

'If I ever need any help from you, I'll be the first to ask for it,' she said in a sneering tone of voice.

* * *

It was the first night of the summer term. Julia went into Jessie's cubicle, in one of the dormitories, thinking that she was asleep, and took back the gold pill box which Mark had originally given her. Jessie waited for her to leave and went straight to Miss Armstrong's study.

The following day, Miss Armstrong summoned Julia to her study. Julia told her the whole story.

'I'd like you to regard me as your friend, Julia,' said the housemistress. Her tone, though intensely sympathetic, was a trifle creepy. Julia wondered whether she had lesbian tendencies. However, she was relieved by having authority as an ally and her eyes became dewy.

'Don't worry. I understand what happened,' said Miss Armstrong. Her tone of voice was rather intimate. Julia shuddered.

'I hope you slept all right, Julia,' said Jessie to Julia, later on that day.

'Don't ever come near me again! You're a bloody sneak, together with a lot of other bloody things,' shouted Julia.

Julia was in tears when Marcia found her sitting on the windowsill in the corridor, outside the house study.

'Your father?' asked Marcia abruptly, her arms straight by her sides.

Julia told her the story which she had told Miss Armstrong but this time so disinterestedly that it sounded phoney.

'It's the most fantastic story I've ever heard. Old Cat Face is an exceptionally nice girl. Besides, almost everyone in the house has had the Oppenheimer brothers.'

'Who's had them?' demanded Julia urgently.

'Oh, I'm not prepared to give names.'

65

'I resent that. Who's had them?' Julia repeated. She added, 'Have *you* had either of them?"

'Shan't say,' said Marcia defiantly.

A bitter but temporary rift ensued between Marcia and Julia. The group split up. Ruth and Miranda remained with Julia, but Marcia and Jessie went off on their own together.

'I went to stay with the Wentridge family during the Easter holidays. Did Julia say anything about all that?' asked Jessie. (She and Marcia were in the house study revising for their 'O' levels.)

Marcia used a humorous approach to hide her divided loyalties.

'She did indeed, Cat Face. From what I heard, it hardly sounds as if your behaviour was impeccable. However, I judge you by what you are like to me.'

Until the girls were due to take their 'O' levels, Marcia kept herself occupied by studying and doing Jessie's French and Latin translations. Jessie was busy writing music and washing, ironing and mending Marcia's clothes, as if she were her maid.

* * *

It was just after the girls had taken their 'O' levels that a strange and terrible thing happened to Marcia, a thing so dreadful that even Jessie's friendship and constant availability were insufficient to save her from mental collapse. Jessie herself had already become heavily involved with heroin and liquor to come to terms with her perpetual unhappiness at school and at home. However, Marcia had been relatively happy with her lot until she became mixed up with something far more harmful than Jessie's drug-taking. She discovered Russian literature.

She read Dostoevsky's *The Brothers Karamazov* when she was ill with food poisoning. The tormented contradictions of the Russian spirit started off as a quirkish fascination, and because Marcia was relatively stable, she thought that the emotions which they inspired in her were within her control. They were not, however. They began to distress and disturb her.

From *The Brothers Karamazov*, she developed an undiscriminating and morbid fascination for all things Russian because she had always had a marked taste for the moribund and the macabre, a trait which she found in fatalistic Russian literature. Marcia had inherited her taste for the macabre from her maternal grandmother who had attended the trial of Crippen when chopped-up pieces of his wife's body were being passed round the jury.

Marcia became Tolstoy's Anna Karenina and sometimes felt like committing suicide by throwing herself under a train. She became Natasha and even Pierre in turn.* She became Pushkin's Tatyana.† She became Maxim Gorki's Foma Gordyev who deteriorated from riches to the madhouse. She had already become Dmitri Karamazov and when she was foolish enough to pick up *Crime and Punishment*, she underwent a sinister metamorphosis into Raskolnikov, which was so overpowering that she walked about with her

---

* Characters from Tolstoy's novel, *War and Peace*.
† See *Yevgeni Onegin*.

67

shoulders furtively hunched and a brown paper parcel under her arm, actually believing that she had murdered the pawnbroker and her companion.

Added to heroin, Jessie had been taking amphetamines which left her, if for a short period of time, in synthetic high spirits. She was working on her opera of *Jane Eyre* night and day and was occasionally going without sleep for a fortnight. She was so heavily drugged that her treatment of Mr Rochester's guise as a gypsy was inadvertently plagiarized from Schubert's *March Militaire* which she thought she had written herself.

'Why do you always have to go round with that ridiculous thing under your arm?' asked Jessie one morning after the girls had had their breakfast.

'I can't live with myself any more. I've turned into someone else. I killed someone to see if I dared to do so. I was all right until about six weeks ago. My peace of mind's been taken away from me and it seems as if I'm never going to get it back,' replied Marcia. Jessie thought for a while before answering.

'I haven't known peace of mind since I lost my father when I was five years old, but I've got used to it. I don't understand why you're taking this extraordinary Russian kick so seriously. Incidentally, what's all this other business? Who have you killed?'

'I just can't get rid of it.'

'What can't you just get rid of?' asked Jessie impatiently.

'A terrible nothingness.'

'You've got to grow up, Marcia,' said Jessie angrily. 'All

intelligent people feel like that from time to time. I feel like it the whole time but, all the same, there are some good things to appreciate in life, like culture, music, friendship and children. Life doesn't consist entirely of novels written by *fucking* Dostoevsky.

Marcia laughed hysterically. There was no joy in her laughter. Then she thought for a while.

'Will it pass, Cat Face?' she asked eventually.

'Will what pass?'

'This ghastly melancholia.'

'No, of course it won't pass. Once it hits you, it stays with you till you croak. I've learnt to live with it since I was five years old, as I said. So can you.'

Marcia felt that Jessie understood a fair amount of what she had been telling her but she knew that there was much of her psyche which she could not communicate to her friend, and her misery was now accompanied by a terrifying feeling of loneliness.

One afternoon, Jessie was wearing her Sunday dress and was due to play Mozart's Sonata Number 11 in the school concert just after the evening meal. She walked arrogantly onto the stage and bowed, staring contemptuously at her audience. Throughout the sonata she kicked her page turner, a slow-witted, somewhat pathetic junior called Mary Eccles, in the shins.

Jessie stormed up to Mary after the concert.

'Do you know one end of a piano from the other?' she shouted.

'Yes, Cat Face!'

'Well, nobody would think so. You're a stupid, poorly educated brat! Added to that, I resent your calling me Cat Face. It's not as if you were a friend of mine.'

Marcia overheard the exchange but felt no pity for Mary. There was no fate in life equal to that of having become Raskolnikov and she too despised Mary because she was jealous of her ignorance and stupidity.

Marcia had become so consistently miserable that she kept a bottle of whisky in her bedside drawer in her dormitory. She shared the dormitory with three other girls, none of whom particularly liked her. She told herself that she wasn't going to read *Crime and Punishment* once the lights had been turned out but the book drew her towards it like a magnet.

She lay in bed on her stomach, reading the book with the aid of a torch. Even the comical scene at the police station failed to impress on her that there is a funny side to all things grave. When Raskolnikov wandered through the back streets of St Petersburg to make himself feel even more depressed than he was already and finally collapsed, physically and psychologically exhausted in his garret, Marcia wept silently. Combined with her tears were hysterical, joyless giggles, brought on by the memory of a reassuringly practical, common-sense inundated man called Barrus Elliott, a passionate sailing man who was typically British and whom she had met at a dance the previous weekend.

He had referred to a passage in which Raskolnikov was accounted for as being 'terribly worried'. (He was worried about the disagreeable Luzhin's forthcoming marriage to Raskolnitov's sister as he bitterly disapproved of him.)

'Terribly worried? Terribly bloody worried?' Barrus had exclaimed in an exasperated tone of voice, adding, 'Why didn't the bugger just build a boat and put to sea, boom, boom, boom boom?'

'How on earth could he have done that?' Marcia had asked.

'Very easily. He could have carried the timbers up to his garret and lowered them through the window on a block 'n tackle.'

The combined action of convulsive laughter and sobbing failed to lesson Marcia's torment. She was too terrified of herself to read any more of *Crime and Punishment*. She rolled on to her back and reached for her bottle of whisky.

'For Christ's sake shut up, Ford!' shouted someone in the dormitory.

'Yes, Ford, you're making a bloody awful noise, opening and shutting drawers. Some of us are trying to sleep.

Marcia struggled to hide her tears from her voice.

'I'm doing my best.'

'None of us are interested in your blasted, bloody best, Ford. Shut the hell up, will you!'

Raskolnikov was round Marcia's neck like a noose. She took a razor blade from her drawer and opened an artery on her wrist, but as the blood gushed out she was suddenly petrified of dying in case she went to hell pursued by Raskolnikov. She wrapped a pillow case and a towel round her arm and went out to find Jessie. She knew that Jessie would tell her what to do.

Miss Armstrong appeared from nowhere. Her ill-fitting games clothes and closely cropped grey hair made her look like an ageing lesbian. Many of the girls in Churchill House suspected her of being a lesbian, although there was no evidence that she was a practising one.

'Heigh-ho, where do you think you're going?' she demanded.

'To the bathroom. I'm not well.'

'No, you weren't. You were going to find Jessie whom you call Cat Face. I can tell you now, she is in the sanatorium following an overdose of amphetamines,' said Miss Armstrong, but Marcia was too preoccupied with Raskolnikov to ask how she was.

'What are all those funny things on your arm?' asked the housemistress.

'Oh, I don't think they're really anything in particular,' replied Marcia inanely.

'What do you mean – you don't think they're really anything in particular? Heigh-ho, you'd better come and see me in my study,' said Miss Armstrong irritably.

A fire burned in Miss Armstrong's grate although it was high summer. Marcia felt light-headed. The whisky had dislodged her depression but hadn't lifted it. She looked at the photograph of the institution for incontinent boys on the mantelpiece and cheered up a little. For all Raskolnikov's shortcomings, there had been no mention in *Crime and Punishment* of him being incontinent. She laughed out loud.

Miss Armstrong knew how to deal with tiresome girls but she had no idea how to deal with people who were totally incomprehensible. She remained standing, banging her right fist into her left palm as she spoke. Marcia sat down.

'It has been reported to me that you sing the Russian national anthem in your bath,' said the butch housemistress angrily.

Marcia felt so disturbed that she no longer cared whether she laughed out loud or not. She laughed again.

'I would thank you not to laugh when I am speaking to you. It creates a most rude impression. Indeed, this is the second time you have laughed since you have been in this room,' said Miss Armstrong irritably.

'I can't help it.'

'A person who laughs for no apparent reason is a simple person. It has also been brought to my attention that you spend a lot of your spare time reading novels by Dostoevsky. Would you discontinue this practice, please. It will make you sicker in the head than you are already.'

'I can't stop it. I'd like to be able to stop it more than anything else in the world. I feel like an alcoholic who longs to stop drinking.'

Another wave of anger surged through Miss Armstrong.

'You thought you could possess Dostoevsky, didn't you? Heigh-ho, you have failed. He has possessed you. He wrote about grim souls in a grim age.'

Marcia was more frightened of herself than of Miss Armstrong's anger and she began to shake.

'What is all that blood doing on my carpet?' asked Miss Armstrong suddenly.

'I'm afraid I've slashed one of my wrists.'

'Heigh-ho, I suppose I'd better call for an ambulance.'

'I want to be with Jessie. Will she be all right?'

'She has had to have a stomach pump. She took an overdose of amphetamines, as I said earlier. We feel she will survive. I don't think your friendship with her is any more suitable than your bizarre literary pursuits.'

'I'm so frightened. I'm terrified of dying and of Raskolnikov living with me in hell for the rest of eternity,' wailed Marcia.

The older woman got even more irritable.

'Heigh-ho, I simply can't keep up with your peculiar peccadilloes. Who the blazes is Raskolnikov?'

Marcia suddenly had hysterical giggles, but she stretched out her hand to Miss Armstrong, believing that she alone could keep her alive. An ambulance siren was heard outside in the drive. Marcia clung to the older woman's sleeve while she looked on, jaded, baffled and exasperated. Miss Armstrong followed Marcia outside.

'Heigh-ho, you really *are* an eccentric young woman!' she shouted as the ambulance came to a halt in the drive.

Once inside the ambulance, Marcia lost consciousness.

She was given a blood transfusion in hospital following a near-fatal suicide attempt and was transferred to the school sanatorium which was nice and airy. It had a pleasant view of the woods nearby. Marcia occupied a bed next to Jessie's in a ward in which six other girls were convalescing. Marcia's mother, Lady Tess Ford, was standing over her, holding a bag. She had chestnut-coloured hair, large brown eyes, unlike her daughter's, a small aquiline nose and was wearing a leopard-skin raincoat over a red dress. She was well-known for her beautiful profile and had been a model when she was young.

'Hullo, darling, I hear you had rather a nasty accident,' she said.

Marcia turned over with her back to her mother. It was not apparent whether Tess was being good humoured and protective, or angry. Her voice was even more strident than Marcia's and when she cleared her throat, which she did at regular intervals due to her asthma, she sounded like a combination of a wounded horse neighing and a gang of Hell's Angels trying to start their motorbikes.

'I've just had a long rambling letter from your head-mistress, followed by an even more prosaic lecture from your housemistress, who, incidentally, struck me as being absolutely half-witted. However, they are both adamant that I come over here and take the Dostoevskys away,' said Tess with a tone of mild irritation in her voice.

'Yes.'

Tess cleared her throat loudly once more and the girls started in their beds.

'Really, darling, there are no two ways about it. They've simply got to go. I'm going up to the house where I will put them all into this bag. Incidentally, they don't belong to you anyway, but to me. They are part of a priceless, pink satin-bound set which your grandfather left me in his will. When I discovered that they were missing, your father and I were naturally very worried and we called the police at once. If you'd asked me in the beginning, this whole dreadful thing would never have happened.'

'I wish I'd never touched them. He's made me so ill,' said Marcia.

Her mother cleared her throat yet again. This time, the girls put their fingers in their ears.

'I think Dostoevsky's a beastly little man. He ought to be resurrected and slain alive,' said Tess obscurely, her voice raised.

Jessie laughed out loud but Marcia had lost her sense of humour.

'I feel worse than I've ever felt in my life. *Crime and Punishment*'s the worst. Am I going to get over it?'

'Yes, of course you're going to get over it, darling. I've brought you some lovely Georgette Heyers. They're much more cheerful than frowsty old Dostoevsky. What about your friend in the next bed? Aren't you going to introduce us?'

'This is Jessie Cavendish. We call her Cat Face. Cat Face, this is my mother,' said Marcia guardedly.

'Hullo, Cat Face. I'm so grateful to you for all the help you've given Marcia. You've been so kind to her.'

'Thank you, Lady Tess.'

'No. Just "Tess". You must come and stay with us in the summer holidays, Cat Face. I shall have to fatten you up,' she said.

Marcia remembered what Julia had told her and the strain of having Jessie to stay was too much for her to bear.

'I don't think that would be a very good idea, Mummy,' she eventually managed to mutter.

'Don't be so inhospitable, darling. Of course it would be convenient for Cat Face to come and stay with us. We've got a perfectly decent swimming pool and a tennis court. What's the point of either if neither is used?'

Tess took a box of chocolates from her bag and left them on the table between the two girls.

'I'm sorry about all this business, Mummy,' said Marcia guiltily.

'So am I. Daddy and I are both terribly upset. We've been in the headmistress's study for forty-five minutes. He found her so formidable that he fainted. Anyway, I've been told to take the Dostoevskys away and that's what I'm going to do,' said Tess assertively.

* * *

Marcia and Jessie planned to stay at Waltham Abbey for a further two years, Marcia to take her 'A' levels in English, French and Latin and Jessie to prepare herself for the Royal Academy of Music. Miranda left at the end of the summer term after her 'O' levels to do a secretarial course, and Buffy Dwyer left in order to train to become an air hostess. Ruth and Julia left to take their 'A' levels at a crammer in London before entering university. Julia intended to read English at Oxford.

Jessie remained outwardly cheerful but inwardly as gloomy and pessimistic as ever. Marcia forced herself to appear cheerful but continued her lugubrious obsession about Russian literature, until one day when another very strange thing happened to her.

She read Maxim Gorki's novel *The Mother*.

A product of a right-wing newspaper family, Marcia had until then remained a staunch and unquestioning Tory. She had thought extensively about the tsarist regime in Russia and had concluded that militant and unwavering autocracy alone could have saved the country from revolution. She felt that this would never have occurred had Nicholas the Second's autocratic father, Alexander the Third, been on the throne in 1917, and also had Rasputin not become involved with Nicholas the Second's family, due to the Tsarevich's haemophilia.

Although Marcia was not an overt reactionary herself, she held a romantic belief in the status quo of tsarist society. She reasoned that it was basically unjust, but she also felt that there was a mystique about it which she thought should not be broken.

It was her conflict between her belief in the status quo and her passion for infectious rebelliousness in the works of some anti-tsarist authors that confused her because the books which she read appeared both right and wrong. It was this confusion more than mere expressions of nihilistic dark spirits that tortured her.

Gorki's *The Mother* and its crude, sentimental, editorializing tones suddenly and very abruptly shattered Marcia's belief in the mystique of tsarist autocracy. Always at either one extreme or another, she ceased being a Tory and became a communist overnight. She had always been exceptionally gullible. Fatalistic themes in pre-revolutionary Russian literature ceased to depress her, since they represented the pursuit of positive change. She began to read communist propaganda sheets and actually believed that Soviet Russia was an earthly paradise to which she longed to emigrate like her heroes, Guy Burgess and Kim Philby.

She found Jessie in the corridor outside the library and told her about her spiritual discovery.

'I feel so much better now, Cat Face. I'm no longer depressed. I've become a communist and I'm going to join the Party. Isn't it wonderful?'

Jessie was not interested in politics. All she cared about was writing music and searching for her next fix of heroin. However, she remembered, not without bitterness, that she had ceased to be happy once she had run away from a communist country.

She communicated her feelings to Marcia and a bond, far deeper than ever before, developed between the two girls. However, Marcia was so engrossed in her new, happy thoughts that she had no idea that Jessie was injecting herself with heroin twice a day to combat the nihilism of her own soul. It was unknown how Jessie found the money to pay for her heroin. Perhaps she stole it.

'I've got an idea, Cat Face,' Marcia said. (They were sitting by themselves in the bootroom.) 'Once we leave school, we'll go to the Soviet Embassy and we'll apply to become Soviet citizens. We'll abandon all our roots in England. You can go to the Moscow Conservatory to study music. Then we can go and work on a collective farm and sing revolutionary songs by a camp fire in the evenings.'

Jessie hadn't even heard the rubbish Marcia had been talking, however. Her shivers and cramps were starting. She put on her coat and disappeared into the town nearby to find some more heroin.

* * *

On a hot July day, towards the end of the summer term, a middle-aged parson, called the Reverend Sydney Baxter, visited Waltham Abbey to conduct the Sunday morning service. His sermon passed vaguely from one subject to another and failed to hold anyone's attention. The Reverend Baxter told the girls to kneel while the headmistress, Miss Heathcote-Barrow, knelt at a pew behind him, dressed demurely in a dark brown, cotton dress with a round white collar. She was wearing a gold crucifix round her neck.

'Let us pray for the American soldiers in Vietnam,' said the Reverend Baxter.

A shrill, savage voice suddenly reverberated from the back of the chapel.

'What about the *fucking* North Vietnamese soldiers?' (It was Jessie's voice.)

There was a silence which lasted for about three minutes. Miss Heathcote-Barrow looked as if she had been lashed across the face with a cold wet towel. She rose to her feet but had to hold on to her pew in order to steady herself.

Very slowly, she walked forward until she became level with the Reverend Baxter. When she spoke, her voice was louder than thunder.

'Jessie Cavendish, you will report to me in my study immediately. Reverend, would you please continue the service.'

Miss Heathcote-Barrow's study was oak-panelled and gaunt. Old school photographs, cups and trophies stood on occasional tables and stags' heads protruded from the walls. A life-sized portrait of the headmistress's late father, Horatio Heathcote-Barrow, was hanging over the grate and on another wall was a large crucifix. Miss Heathcote-Barrow's voice was powerful, resonant and daunting.

'Jessie Rose Cavendish, it is not my intention to nauseate these walls by going into detail about the hideous and repellent behaviour which you have just displayed. You are a walking, infested anathema to the noble ideals for which this school stands, stood and ever more shall stand.

'Were this outrage committed by another girl, it would have been a question of instant expulsion. But for you, expulsion would be a treat, not a punishment. However, you will forfeit all your outings for the next three terms.'

Jessie looked at the life-sized portrait of Horatio Heathcote-Barrow. She observed that both the father and the daughter had the same sallow complexion, prominent cheekbones and small brown eyes. Jessie was completely undaunted by her.

'As your headmistress and guardian, I am responsible for the salvation of your soul and there is one question that the responsibilities of my station demand that I ask,' continued Miss Heathcote Barrow.

Jessie stood with her hands clasped behind her back and her head bowed.

'Are you a communist, Jessie?'

Jessie raised her head and looked the headmistress straight in the eye.

'Yes.'

The headmistress crossed herself. She looked briefly at her father's portrait, as if to seek guidance from him, and raised her eyes to the ceiling.

'You realize that there is no place for a communist in the Kingdom of Heaven,' she said eventually.

'I don't understand that,' said Jessie, adding, 'Christ is reputed to have said that it is harder for a rich man to enter the Kingdom of Heaven than it is for a camel to pass through the eye of a needle. Only a communist would make a remark like that.

'Not a communist, Jessie, a socialist maybe. Christ lived in a cruel and repressive society, in which it was acceptable to be a socialist. Had he been born in England, he would have been a patriot and a Tory.

Jessie was becoming bored with the conversation. She needed another heroin injection fast. She tried to take her mind off her increasing stomach cramps and wondered whether she could get away with using variations of the theme of the *Toasting Aria* from *Carmen* for Jane Eyre's reunion with Mr Rochester.

Miss Heathcote-Barrow interrupted her thoughts.

'Marxist ideology states that religion is the opium of the people. Is that your belief?'

'Yes.'

The headmistress's eyes filled with tears.

'I feel that your soul may be completely beyond redemption. Do you know of any other girls in the school who are tainted?'

'Tainted?'

'Who are communists?'

'No.'

'Have you not spoken to any of them about your beliefs?'

The symptoms of heroin withdrawal had completely obliterated what little fear was generated from Miss Heathcote-Barrow to Jessie.

'I keep myself to myself. I've got my music to write. I'm far too busy to piss about talking to people about fucking Karl Marx,' replied Jessie cheekily.

Miss Heathcote-Barrow looked as if someone had punched her in the jaw. It took her a while to compose herself, and when she spoke her voice was faint and sepulchral.

'A portrait of the last Archbishop of Canterbury in his ceremonial robes hangs on one wall, Jessie, and a life-sized crucifix on the other. I would thank you to moderate your language', said Miss Heathcote-Barrow, adding, 'tell me about the Ford girl. Is she a communist?'

'I've got absolutely no idea. Why don't you ask her?'

'I feel in the circumstances that there is only one choice open to us, which is to kneel down and pray.'

Jessie was astounded. The cramps in her stomach and pronounced shivers were becoming intolerable.

'What, now?'

'There is no alternative. Time is of the essence.'

They both knelt. Tears rolled down Miss Heathcote-Barrow's cheeks as she spoke.

'Almighty God, I beseech thee in thy most infinite wisdom to have mercy on thy servant, Jessie Cavendish, and to deliver her from iniquity unto the paths of righteousness, through the bounteous majesty of thy son, Jesus Christ, our Lord.'

The headmistress and Jessie both said 'amen' softly. Miss Heathcote-Barrow staggered to her feet and stumbled into a chair as if she were about to have a heart attack. Jessie fought desperately to keep a straight face, despite her extreme discomfort.

'Go now, Jessie, I need to be alone,' said the headmistress.

The ceiling of the long, sombre-looking corridor outside the headmistress's study was supported by imposing Gothic arches. As Jessie walked along it urgently, Marcia emerged from the library, waving the *Thoughts of Chairman Mao* in the air, laughing out loud. She was cold, despite the time of year, and was wearing a coat and scarf. The central heating in the school had been turned off because it was the summer term.

'Hey, Cat Face!'

Jessie's shivers and cramps brought on by heroin withdrawal were getting even worse than they had been in the headmistress's study. She was looking pained and gaunt.

'What happened, Cat Face? Did she give you the chop?'

Jessie glared at Marcia with brutal harshness which terrified her.

'Give me your coat and scarf. Don't waste my time. I've got to go into the town,' she shouted.

'You were terrific, Cat Face, shouting that in front of the whole school. I've never seen such guts in my life.'

'Shut up, Marcia! Didn't you hear what I said? Give me your coat and scarf.'

'You've got a temperature, haven't you? You don't need to go anywhere. I'll help you up to bed. I'll get you something from the chemist.'

'Didn't you hear what I said? Get out of my bloody way!'

'Cool it, Cat Face.'

Jessie slapped Marcia across the face and Marcia burst into tears.

'Why are you being so hostile? You've hurt me, Cat Face. I thought I was your pal.'

'Are you going to give me your coat and scarf or am I going to have to rip them off your back?'

Marcia handed them over. The incident shocked her so much that she convinced herself that she had fallen asleep in the library and had had a bad dream.

* * *

It was ten o'clock the following morning, which a Monday. Marcia was sitting in the crowded library reading *The Daily Worker*, later to become *The Morning Star*, which she had bribed the cleaning woman, Mrs Bray, to bring her, with half a crown* every morning. She was still

*Old English currency.

wondering whether her previous encounter with Jessie had been real or a dream.

Jessie suddenly appeared with a bundle of music sheets under her arm. She no longer looked pale and haggard but pink-cheeked and healthy. The heroin injection, which she had just given herself in one of the school's lavatories, had brought on an abrupt, if temporary, transformation in her. Marcia had become convinced that her experience the day before had been a bad dream. She had no idea that Jessie was using heroin.

'Hullo, Marce!'

'Cat Face, I've been very worried about you. I had an awful dream. You were so mean and disagreeable. You hit me.'

'Come on, Marce, you can't judge someone by what they do in a dream,' said Jessie cheerfully.

'What did H-B say to you in her study?' asked Marcia.

'Oh she just bumbled on and on about my fucking immortal soul. She made me kneel down and pray.'

'*What?*' Marcia thought for a while. 'I always thought that she was eccentric but I had no idea that she was bonkers.'

'Let's see *The Daily Worker*, Marce. Is there anything new in it?' asked Jessie.

When Marcia read *The Daily Worker*, she liked to spread it across the whole table with its front page raised so that its title could be seen by girls sitting at other tables. She always glued herself to it with an expression of earnest determination, underlining things and turning the pages reverently, as if the very paper on which the newspaper was printed were sacred. She folded it neatly and passed it to Jessie. She had once been reprimanded by her mother, Lady Tess Ford, in an upmarket Mayfair hairdresser's. Marcia had been reading *The Daily Worker* under the drier and her mother had snatched it from her and torn it up, much to the amusement of a few of the hairdressers.

'I don't think we'll be seeing *her* in here again,' one of the hairdressers had remarked unpleasantly. This had only increased Tess's embarrassment.

'I do have an *awful* lot to put up with,' she had muttered in a sepulchral tone of voice.

'There's always something new in *The Daily Worker.* Part of today's editorial is about Vietnam. The other part's about Rhodesia,' uttered Marcia in a loud whisper.

Jessie glossed over the editorials and turned to the last page.

'There's a form here inviting readers to join the Communist Party,' she said.

'Yes, I know, I've already joined. They sent me a card after I had given them a cheque for seven and six.* They wanted to come and see me to talk things over. I gave my address as Churchill House, Stoke Hill, but I didn't say anything about Waltham Abbey. They sent me a polite letter addressed to "Dear Comrade Ford", saying that they couldn't find my house. It wouldn't be quite the thing to get them wandering round a public school, looking for me, so I said I wasn't living at any fixed address because I was travelling round the country, trying to get in touch with the proletariat.'

*Old English currency – seven shillings and sixpence.

Jessie gave her well-known neighing laugh while the other girls in the library shushed for silence. Marcia and Jessie ignored them.

Marcia tore the form inviting people to join the Communist Party out of the newspaper and showed it to Jessie.

'I've suddenly got a brilliant idea,' she said.

'Enlighten me, dear heart,' said Jessie.

'Let's fill this form in in H-B's name, giving her private address. We could send some communists round there.'

'Oh, do do that. It would be so funny!'

Caroline Baines, the Head of School, with disfiguring acne and a mane of lustrous blonde hair, tied back in a navy blue velvet ribbon, came over to the table at which Marcia and Jessie were sitting.

'This is a library, not a pub. You've got no business making all this noise in here. Hand over that newspaper.'

Marcia smiled slyly and handed it over. It was as if she were handing over part of herself. When Caroline saw the newspaper's title, she rattled it furiously in the air as if it were a filthy dishcloth, impregnated with excrement.

'This is a communist newspaper. You know perfectly well that communist newspapers are not allowed in this school.'

'I *am* a communist,' said Marcia in a raised voice so that everyone in the library could hear her words.

'In that case, you've got no business being at this school.'

Jessie was giggling helplessly.

'You appear to find it funny that Marcia Ford is a communist. You wouldn't find it so funny if you lived behind the Iron Curtain where people who are not communists are sentenced to twenty-five years' hard labour,' said Caroline angrily.

'I spent the first five years of my life behind what you call the Iron Curtain and they were the only happy years I knew,' said Jessie.

'In that case, why don't you go back there?'

'There wouldn't be much point. The only blood relation I had there was my father and I believe he was shot at the Austrian frontier. I am a Hungarian refugee.'

Jessie started crying and Marcia put her arm round her.

'You will leave this library, the pair of you. You are both thoroughly undesirable,' said the Head of School assertively.

* * *

'What about the form in *The Daily Worker*? Are you going to fill it in again?' asked Jessie.

She and Marcia were sitting in an alcove off one of the classrooms which the two girls used for smoking cannabis and drinking neat whisky.

'I've already filled it in in H-B's name. I've even forged her signature. Have a look. It's absolutely hilarious,' said Marcia, who took a swig of whisky and passed the bottle to Jessie.

'I know her address,' said Marcia, adding, 'it's the Manor House, Whitchurch Road, near Amersham, Buckingham-shire. She's even got a chapel attached to her house. When she sees someone asking her to join the Communist Party, she's going to have a heart attack.'

The girls were hopelessly drunk and stoned and were laughing and joking. They were making a fiendish racket.

'Are you still screwing my father's chauffeur, Cat Face?' asked Marcia, her voice raised.

''Course I am, stupid!'

'I bet he's not half as good as his son. His son's brilliant.'

'I'll take your word for it. How are you getting on with that hilarious poem which you were writing about the midwife who delivered Lenin?'

'I've only written the first two verses so far.' Marcia began to recite, her speech slurred.

> *Screaming in pain, she in agony heaved.*
> *Heavily sweating, she heavily breathed,*
> *As a mother lay down and gave birth to a son.*
> *As the waters gushed out, a new era began*
> *On the twenty-second of April.*

> *And I it was who heated the coal,*
> *To boil the water for the old mare's foal,*
> *Who brought out the forceps to open the hole,*
> *And I it was who supplied the towels,*
> *And I it was who supplied the bucket,*
> *And I it was who had the honour to tie a knot*
> *in the cord and cut it.*

'I'm going to send it to the Soviet Embassy and ask them if someone can translate it into Russian so that it can be published in *Pravda*,'* announced Marcia.

Jessie was convulsed. Marcia loved nothing more than

*The mouthpiece of the Communist Party in Soviet Russia.

an audience. She continued, 'I've also managed to complete my pornographic short story about two Red Army soldiers. It's entitled, *Sergei Pitched and Andrei Caught*. I'll read some of it to you. Listen to this.' Marcia produced a piece of paper and began to read aloud, her eyes rolling in their sockets like a madman's.

Sergei Alexandrovich and Andrei Ignatevich walked hand in hand from their commune on to the site of a factory which had recently been bombed by the Germans. They had just shot some evil traitors and a beautiful blood-red bond united them and stirred their loins. High on a wall, miraculously unscathed, was a giant portrait of their beloved Ilyich.* Its beauty surged through their blood like an opiate. The comrades threw themselves to the ground in desperate abandon.

'Give me your backside, Andrei, there's a dear,' said Sergei Alexandrovich.

Andrei Ignatevich felt as if he were being buggered by the noble Ilyich in person. Tears of glory poured down his cheeks and red hot history, gold as flowing, liquid fire, surged through his bowels as he and his comrade swung into the 'Internationale'.

'Marcia, that's a bloody terrible piece of writing!' exclaimed Jessie.

'I haven't polished it up yet. I've started to write another poem which begins with the words,

*Vladimir Ilyich Lenin's name is frequently abbreviated to 'Ilyich' by hardline communists.

91

Aloof on the shore, stands a Soviet worker, one of the lords of wisdom.

Humbly, he stoops to wash his hands in the raging but soothing waters,

but I haven't yet worked out what to do with it after that,' said Marcia, adding, 'I know a communist in London who's writing a book about homosexual rights. His name's Jamie Landau. He's asked me to think of a title for his book. He says it must be left wing in tone as well as being supportive of homosexuality.'

'Well, what about *Class and the Arse?* or *A Working Man's Arse is his Castle?* Or better still, *A Working Man's Guide to the Tradesman's Entrance?*' suggested Jessie naively.

Marcia giggled loudly. 'Last weekend, Jamie suggested that he and I attend a Communist Party meeting, so I went along with him.' She continued, 'He's got a blistering public school accent, which is more potent than a tropical midday sun. He went up to this old cloth-capped gaffer, slapped him on the back and shouted, "I say, comrade, I think *The Daily Worker's* a *fucking* good newspaper, what!" The dandruff from under the astounded gaffer's cap cascaded onto his shoulders.'

Jessie cackled even more loudly than before. She sounded like a banshee being buried alive.

Suddenly, the two girls heard Caroline Baines's voice shouting from outside the alcove.

'Come out of there!'

Marcia and Jessie were silent.

'I know you're in there.'

The girls came out.

'You've been drinking alcohol, haven't you?' said Caroline. '*And* smoking dope.'

'No, we haven't,' said Jessie.

'Show me the bottle.'

'We haven't got a bottle.'

'I overheard most of your conversation. I think you're both absolutely disgusting. Where are you supposed to be now?'

Marcia waved her arms theatrically in the air and stared rudely at Caroline.

'In a troika borne by thunderous snow-white steeds across a boundless steppe, scattering uplifting Marxist literature to the winds and singing the "Internationale"!' she exclaimed.

'That was an extremely frivolous answer, Marcia Ford. Jessie Cavendish, you will learn fourteen lines from Shakespeare's *Richard III*, and Marcia, you will learn twenty-eight lines for being so damned impertinent.'

* * *

The Manor House, lived in by Miss Heathcote-Barrow (H-B), was a few miles away from Waltham Abbey School. It had been given to her by her father. The chapel, which was attached, had simple whitewashed arches inside it and a single pew close to the altar. The glass in the windows was plain because Miss Heathcote-Barrow liked plenty of natural light, whenever she visited the chapel. It somehow made her feel closer to her maker.

It was a Saturday morning during the summer holidays.

It was early August. She was kneeling and praying out loud. She was reciting a prayer: 'Our Father, who art in heaven . . .'

' 'Scuse me, Miss.'

She was not expecting visitors. She turned round and sprang to her feet.

The man she saw was about twenty-five years old with inky black shoulder-length hair, parted in the centre, secured by an off-white Vietnamese mourning band. He was wearing a shabby denim jacket and matching denim jeans tucked into worn-out cowboy boots.

'Who are you and what do you want?' asked Miss Heathcote-Barrow. There was a tone of fear in her voice.

'Hermione Heathcote-Barrow?' The visitor's voice was loud and harsh and his accent was local.

'This is she.'

'I've come about your application to join the Communist Party.'

'*The Communist Party?*' gasped Miss Heathcote-Barrow.

'I'll thank you not to be dismissive with me.'

The visitor, a communist, whose name was Dave Thompson, reached into his pocket and pulled out the completed form with Miss Heathcote-Barrow's forged signature on it.

'This is your signature, isn't it? Hermione Heathcote-Barrow?'

'It looks as if it is but it must be a forgery. I come from a family of upright muscular Christians. My late father was the Archbishop of Canterbury. I want nothing to do with the Communist Party. Kindly leave,' said the stunned headmistress.

'I don't think you appreciate how much time I've put

94

aside to come and see you. I don't care for your attitude,' said Thompson irritably.

He was ill at ease but he found Miss Heathcote-Barrow's loud commanding voice twistedly attractive. 'Don't be too hard on your poor comrade. Between you and me, I haven't had my oats for over a fortnight. How about a bunk-up?' he asked cheekily.

'*A bunk-up? A bunk-up?*' Miss Heathcote-Barrow's booming voice echoed and reverberated round the chapel. Rage surged through her like a virus. She grabbed hold of a heavy silver cross from near the altar with both hands and wielded it in front of Thompson's face. Thompson lost his temper and wrenched it from her hands and she ran out of the chapel, screaming.

'When we seize power, we'll have you shot, you arrogant, bourgeois old cow!' shouted Thompson.

* * *

Marcia and Jessie waited outside Miss Heathcote-Barrow's study at the beginning of the autumn term. Jessie was hoping she would be expelled but Marcia was terrified because she was determined to complete her 'A' levels.

Once inside the study, their circumstances somehow seemed unreal. Even the walls of the room were livid with rage.

'Jessie Rose Cavendish and Marcia Marion Margaret Ford, the outrage which you have both committed against me and against this school knows no living parallel in the realms of tongue or pen. One of you said that you were going to post a form with my name on it, having forged

95

my signature, stating that I wished to join the Communist Party. You were both overheard planning this evil stunt by someone who happened to be outside an alcove adjoining one of the classrooms towards the end of last term. You will go to your dormitories and house study and assemble your possessions. You are both expelled. I have informed your mothers who are utterly appalled. May the Lord have mercy on your immortal souls.'

As the girls walked along the corridor away from her study, they heard Miss Heathcote-Barrow's voice erupt in a bull-like orgasm of fury.

'Get out of my school!'

* * *

Marcia's father's chauffeur pulled up in the drive and Jessie ran towards him.

'Come on, let's go into the woods. It will be our last time. My friend Marcia Ford and I have just been expelled from the school,' she announced. There was a tone of pride in her voice.

Every girl in Churchill House had gathered in ghoulish fascination. They peered through the opened windows onto the drive outside the house.

'Not a chance, Cat Face, not in front of an audience. I could lose my job.'

The chauffeur went into the building to collect Marcia's heavy trunk which was covered with chalked writing in letters about ten inches high. 'MARCIA FORD. BY CAR.' The chauffeur picked up the trunk and the chalk rubbed off on his recently ironed smart grey trousers. This, together with the end of his affair with Jessie, caused him to be in a foul temper.

'What the flaming 'ell do they think you're going 'ome by? Flippin' aeroplane?' the peppery chauffeur shouted.

* * *

Marcia and Jessie did not keep in touch much after leaving Waltham Abbey, mainly because Jessie did not wish to be reminded of a place where she had been so unhappy. However, when Marcia rang her up the following April and invited her to accompany her to the Soviet Embassy, to deliver flowers there on Lenin's birthday, on the twenty-second of that month, Jessie reluctantly agreed to come along with her.

It was a pleasant sunny spring day. The two girls were admitted to the Embassy and Marcia thrust a bouquet of red carnations into the hands of the astounded man who had opened the door. He was round and stout and bald as a billiard ball and looked like Khrushchev.* He was the first Soviet citizen that Marcia had met. She was in awe of him and spoke in a hushed, deep, monotonous tone of voice.

'We are communists,' she began, 'and we would like to present these flowers to you in honour of our Saviour, namely Comrade Lenin, who was born upon this great and glorious day.'

The man looked puzzled, bored and impassive.

'I don't quite know how to put this to you but I have

*President of the Soviet Union after Stalin's death.

97

written a poem about the midwife who delivered Lenin. In fact, it is entitled *The Midwife who Delivered Lenin*. I sent it to your Embassy some time ago but I got no reply. I am most anxious that you pass it on to your Cultural Attaché in the hope that it will be translated into Russian and published in *Pravda*,' ventured Marcia, her voice trembling.

The man failed to put her at her ease and continued to stare at her, like a baffled owl waiting to be fed. He understood English perfectly.

'I would like you to know that I take my communist beliefs extremely seriously, and with your kind permission, I will read aloud my poem about the midwife who delivered Lenin, which is written on a piece of paper attached to my red carnations,' said Marcia timidly.

Writing poetry had never been Marcia's forte but she was unique in thinking that her poem was brilliant. She read the poem aloud, stressing the last three verses, her voice becoming increasingly lower and even more monotonous, while Jessie scowled at her.

> *I am old and ill and lame.*
> *Today, I tried to get out of a train,*
> *But a coarse, rude ruffian blocked my path,*
> *An enemy of the working class.*
>
> *Who was this anti-Soviet lout,*
> *Who stood in my way when I tried to get out,*
> *When I'd tended the mare and sponged her down,*
> *And slashed the cord when the baby crashed out?*

'Take my sheath knife, comrade', a soldier said.
His face was kindly and his soul was red,
And I lunged straight into the ruffian then,
And I slit his throat, as I slashed the cord.

For some reason totally incomprehensible to Marcia, the man suddenly stared at her with intense hostility and suspicion which graduated to savage hatred.

He shouted hysterically for a while in his native tongue but Marcia couldn't understand what he was saying because she had only recently started to teach herself Russian. As the man's rage reached a climax, he spluttered like a cuckolded colonel and shrieked a single isolated word.

'Poshli!' *

Marcia was extremely hurt but her mental pain turned to fear. She grabbed Jessie by the hand and ran out of the building.

'Why does that man hate me so much, Cat Face? I was only making a friendly gesture towards him and his country. I don't understand,' said Marcia naively. Her voice was trembling, as if she were about to burst into tears.

'Oh, don't you? What the hell did you expect to happen when you read aloud a bloody stupid poem like that, referring to Lenin's mother as an "old mare", and saying that you'd sponged her down?' shouted Jessie, adding, 'Kindly don't call me Cat Face any more. Only my friends call me that!'

'But don't you think my poem's good? You almost

* 'Get out!'

99

encouraged me to write it when we were at school. Don't you remember?'

'No, I don't think your poem's good!' Jessie continued to shout. 'I think it's pathetic, and I also think you're pathetic.' (She was beginning to get cramps due to heroin withdrawal and her temper was worsening.)

'Why do you think I'm pathetic, Jessie?' asked Marcia. Tears were rolling down her cheeks.

'The whole poem's rubbish and it isn't even well-written,' Jessie bellowed, adding, 'babies don't crash out of women's bodies. They slide. Also, Russian soldiers don't hand out bloody sheath knives to old women on trains. Do you think I haven't got anything better to do besides accompany you on your ludicrous and embarrassing adventures? Please don't ring me up any more! You seem to have forgotten that my father was shot by a Russian guard at the Austrian border when I was five years old. I have come to hate communists and I want nothing further to do with you or any other communist. Don't ever contact me again!'

Marcia was deeply hurt and wept for two days. That was the last time she saw Jessie before they met years later on the M4 motorway, when they were both thirty-five years old.

* * *

Jessie was in the habit of going to the Boar's Head pub in Kensington, where she made friends with a hashish smoker called Lady Evangeline Pleasuredog. Evangeline was quite some years her senior. She was fifty-five years old. She was extremely rich and dressed in flowing robes of different colours. She looked like a combination of Lady Ottoline Morrell and Isadora Duncan. She had immaculately dyed blonde hair which was never seen to grow out at the roots. She had it dyed once a week at an expensive London hairdressers'.

The two women decided to go into rehab. Evangeline felt so sorry for Jessie that she offered to pay for her rehab at the Priory Hospital in Roehampton, London, SW15. The Priory is a singularly expensive and unpleasant place. It was known to the two women as the 'White-washed House of Usher' because of its Gothic architecture which was painted white.

Evangeline never failed to delight Jessie because of her loud, resonant, booming voice which would have put many a forlorn Venetian bell bitterly to shame.

Evangeline and Jessie were supervised by the same consultant psychiatrist, Dr Ryan Campbell, who was notorious for being callous, arrogant, heartless and cruel. He was Irish and was later struck off the medical register.

He was very tall and had lank hair falling over his face, slip-on shoes, suggesting that he may have been sexually promiscuous, a watch on a chain across his chest, disfiguring acne on his chin and a handshake as limp as a eunuch's cock. He thought he was God's gift to women.

He was snobbish and his treatment of Jessie was more humiliating than that of Evangeline. He asked Jessie to mount a platform in a room occupied by about twenty-five other psychiatrists, all of whom Jessie thought should have been garroted with piano wire. She was to hear this expression from a woman called Miss Wilberforce whose words she heard at a later date.

'Would you mind giving us your name, please?' Campbell said with mock civility.

'www.jessiecavendish.net,' replied Jessie aggressively, adding, 'don't just sit there, you idle fuckers, write it down!'

Jessie's and Evangeline's rehab was short-lived. They both escaped from the Priory and hailed a taxi outside the hospital. Jessie started to inject herself with heroin once more and Evangeline resumed her habit of smoking hashish.

Evangeline had a twenty-five-year-old son called Douglas-Cyril who was autistic and who was bald and bearded. His behaviour was outrageous. One evening, for reasons best known to himself, he went into a crowded restaurant, turned over a table and shouted '*FUCK!*' at the top of his voice. Jessie found this highly amusing.

Evangeline invited Jessie to stay with her and Douglas-Cyril, in her country house in Sussex. It was the autumn and it was the time of the Harvest Festival. Evangeline and Douglas-Cyril were in a church. The congregation were singing a long hymn, which never seemed to end. For no apparent reason, Douglas-Cyril suddenly swept all the Harvest Festival's paraphernalia off a table onto the floor of the church. He was wearing an off-white baseball cap, a shirt bearing the words 'Let's Castrate Anthony' and a pair of tight leather shorts. Douglas-Cyril's behaviour greatly amused Jessie, so much so that she actually encouraged him to misbehave. (There was a mischievous streak in her melancholic character.) Evangeline frequently bellowed in her loud, booming voice, 'Don't do that, Douglas-Cyril!' but her words fell on deaf ears.

Evangeline told Jessie about her passion for Marseilles, and suggested that she and Douglas-Cyril go there for a holiday with her. Evangeline had been to Marseilles on several occasions and adored the city. She loved its seediness, its bouillabaisse restaurants, surrounding its beautiful harbour, its backstreets cluttered with discarded syringes, its wafts of garlic, the permanent sound of accordions, and the colourful street fights occurring near the harbour and in the back alleys. Most of all, she liked to swim round the harbour, watching the sunset, followed by the reflection of the city's lights on the water when it got dark. Sometimes, she swam across the harbour for kicks. She stated in her will that she wished to have her ashes scattered over Marseilles harbour. Her Trustee, who took her instructions down, was absolutely flabbergasted.

On one occasion, when she was swimming across Marseilles harbour, a gendarme leant out of his boat, narrowly missing her head and furiously shouted the words, '*Madame, que foutez-vous?*', to which Evangeline replied calmly, '*Je nage, monsieur, je nage*'.* Jessie came to adore Marseilles for the same reasons as Evangeline and also swam in the harbour. Her almost permanent gloom lessened when she was there. However, at that time, Douglas-Cyril's autism had become much more severe.

---

* 'Madame, what the fucking hell are you doing?' to which Evangeline replied calmly, 'I am swimming, monsieur, I am swimming.'†
† The author had an identical experience in 1982.

Evangeline and Jessie did not take long to consult a drug dealer and were able to prop themselves up with heroin and hashish. The hashish calmed Evangeline and enabled her to see that Douglas-Cyril's behaviour did not seem too outrageous, if only temporarily.

While the three tourists were walking down one of Marseilles's backstreets one night, after a boozy dinner and a shot of drugs for the two women, they all noticed a brothel called Las Vegas. It was approached by a red carpet on the pavement leading to the building.

Jessie was curious. She wanted to see what a brothel looked like on the inside so she walked straight in. Douglas-Cyril followed her because he wanted a woman. Evangeline begged her autistic son, in her loud, carrying voice, to come outside into the street.

'Douglas-Cyril!' she shouted. 'You never know what you might catch in there. Come out at once!'

Douglas-Cyril ignored his mother. He spoke at the top of his voice, with a pronounced public school accent. He was waving a half bottle of whisky in the air, the other half of which he had consumed.

He made no allowances for the fact that the Madame did not speak English and approached her.

'I say, I require a whore,' he shouted, in his heavy upper-class accent, adding, 'I don't require a predatory whore who lies on top of me when I fuck her. I require a subservient whore who lies underneath me when I fuck her, what!' Jessie greatly enjoyed his nonsensical behaviour.

'You simply *must* come out of there, Douglas-Cyril!'

pleaded Evangeline, but Douglas-Cyril again ignored his mother who was almost as eccentric as he was.

'Would you all go away, please. I'm very busy,' said the Madame mildly (in French). Then Jessie, who spoke fluent French, said something unbelievably rude, which Evangeline could not understand, but which caused the Madame to chase the three of them down the street, brandishing an Oswald Mosley-style knuckleduster.

* * *

The well-off Evangeline owned a large, impeccably decorated house in London, overlooking St Paul's Cathedral. She had a fiery cook called Sinead (pronounced 'Shinade') O'Farrell who was from Dublin.

Jessie knew that Douglas-Cyril always behaved badly and in a disinhibited manner when he was under the influence of alcohol, particularly spirits. For some reason, unbeknown to Jessie, he could tolerate whisky but not gin.

Evangeline invited some of her friends, including Jessie and Douglas-Cyril, to her house in order to celebrate her birthday one evening. Jessie brought a large bottle of gin which she said was a gift for Evangeline. She also brought two ounces of hashish.

Very surreptitiously, Jessie repeatedly topped up Douglas-Cyril's glass with gin, together with an exceptionally small amount of tonic water, before, during and after dinner, longing to watch him misbehave.

However, on this occasion, the more gin he consumed, the more subdued he became. Jessie had been unaware of the fact that although he could hold large quantities of whisky he could not hold the same amount of gin.

Douglas-Cyril stumbled off his chair and crawled into Sinead's bedroom, thinking that it was the bathroom. He then lay on his back on Sinead's bed, making retching noises. Jessie had the presence of mind to rush into Sinead's bedroom, roll him onto his side, and bend his legs in the recovery position. She knew that if he remained on his back, he would have choked to death on his own vomit. He was copiously sick onto the wall, as well as Sinead's bedclothes, the carpet and the clothes that had been strewn on the floor by Sinead.

Jessie, who was responsible for Douglas-Cyril's colossal consumption of gin, went into the dining room and sheepishly explained what had happened to Sinead, rather than Evangeline. She was somewhat scared of Evangeline at this point. She thought she owed it to Sinead to tell her the truth. She found it difficult to speak to her as she was pretty drunk herself, as well as being stoned with heroin.

'Er-um-well,' Jessie ventured haltingly, adding, 'I'm afraid I've got some rather worrying news about Douglas-Cyril.'

'What news?' asked Sinead urgently.

'Well, I don't really know quite how to put this to you,' she began, slurring her words, adding, 'I'm afraid Douglas-Cyril has sort of gone into your bedroom...'

'My bedroom?' exclaimed Sinead.

'Well, he is ever so slightly the worse for wear and he has, well, kind of been taken ill in your bedroom. Er, you'd better come in and see.'

Sinead rushed into her bedroom.

'Jaysus, Mary and Joseph!' she shouted, 'the boy's been sick all over the wall, the bed, the pillows and the floor.'

'Well, yes,' said Jessie, adding, 'He was on his back retching, so I took the liberty of turning him onto his side, facing the wall, so that he wouldn't suffocate.'

Douglas-Cyril had been sick over Sinead's pillows, duvet, mattress, carpet, her clothes which she had thrown on the floor as well as a large part of the wall. Jessie had hysterical giggles.

Sinead lost her temper, handed in her notice, packed her bags and left Evangeline's employ that evening.

'You really have behaved awfully badly,' said Evangeline to Jessie, mildly, adding, 'now I'll have to interview yet another batch of cooks. You don't realize how difficult it is to *find* a decent cook these days.'

* * *

Several months had passed since Marcia's and Jessie's quarrel. It was October and very windy. Jessie had recently won a scholarship to the Royal Academy of Music. Jeanette had laid down a deposit for her tuition, board and lodging but refused to give her any other financial support. Jessie fuelled her heroin addiction by working whenever she could as a temporary medical secretary and a prostitute. She picked up medical terminology from textbooks which she borrowed from the London Library. (Medical secretaries earned far more than ordinary secretaries.)

It was compulsory to attend three tutorials a week at

the Royal Academy of Music. Jessie shared them with two brilliant but conversationally limited girls called Karen Wells and Charlotte Spry and a young man called Malcolm Lowther, a bisexual Scotsman from Edinburgh. He had rugged good looks and a talent for strings, wind and keyboard instruments alike. He had bright green eyes and thick shaggy blond hair. Jessie found him devastatingly attractive.

Keith Johnson supervised the tutorials. He was the Director of the Royal Academy of Music and he enjoyed nationwide fame as a conductor. He was middle-aged, barbed-tongued, white-haired and pompous. He gave easily to rage and was frequently flushed in the face, due to his high blood pressure. He later died of a massive heart attack while conducting the Scherzo movement of Beethoven's Ninth at the Royal Albert Hall.

So far during the tutorial, Lowther had been contributing more to the discussion than his fellow students. Karen and Charlotte contributed too, but not very extensively. Lowther was commenting on orchestration techniques and making cross-references to two operatic masterpieces currently on the syllabus. Johnson was disgruntled by Jessie's silence and addressed his next remark to her.

'In your last exercise, I asked you to orchestrate the *Non Più Andrai* aria from the *Marriage of Figaro* piano score. I found your introduction of trombones and trumpets, ludicrously ahead of Mozart's time, a trifle bombastic, not to mention adolescent. Perhaps you would care to account for it?' he said in a cutting tone of voice.

Gin, heroin and the need for money to support her gin and drugs habit were having an increasingly disruptive effect on Jessie's studies. She did not have cramps this time, however, as she had given herself a heroin injection in one of the Academy's lavatories just before the tutorial.

'I can't account for what I wrote. My concentration's not as good as it was,' she muttered candidly.

'Evidently not,' said Johnson. 'If you insist on wasting my time, the very least you can do is try to show some musicianship.'

'I don't think I've got any fucking musicianship.'

'Then you've got no business studying in this institution. Not only that, I'd thank you to moderate your language.'

Lowther followed Jessie to the canteen after the tutorial and found her in tears.

'I don't think you've ever been afraid of anyone in your life, Jessie,' he said.

'Oh, call me Cat Face.'

'No one at the Academy would dare to say something like that to that bastard, Johnson,' said Lowther.

'I've got nothing to live for so I've got nothing to lose,' said Jessie in a deadpan tone of voice.

Lowther found Jessie's feline face, emaciated features, waist-length jet-black hair and melancholic aura attractive. He persuaded her to come back to his bedsit, where he cooked her a generous pile of lasagne which she couldn't hold down and this intrigued him even more.

The gloomy bedsit which Lowther rented was in Fulham. It was small and dark with magenta-coloured wallpaper peeling off its grimy, cracked walls. There was a matching dark-red bedspread, a dark-red threadbare carpet, an unmade bed with music sheets strewn all over it and a pile of unwashed plates in the corner.

'I don't think you're very well, Cat Face. Why don't you lie down?' ventured Lowther.

Jessie lay down. She had had a heroin injection about an hour before in one of the lavatories at the Academy. Lowther put on a recording of the Birdman's aria towards the end of *The Magic Flute*, the *Ein Mädchen oder Menschen* aria, which comforted and relaxed Jessie. Lowther took the music sheets from his bed and put them on the floor. He lay down by Jessie's side and seduced her. Within six weeks, they got married.

Lowther had no idea that Jessie was addicted to heroin. Jessie was then spending two days a week working as a temporary medical secretary, which encompassed taking dictation from a dictaphone, namely of letters from consultants and their underlings in hospitals and clinics to patients' GPs. When temporary medical secretarial work was slack, Jessie worked as a prostitute.

Jessie's agency, The Medical and General Agency, sent her to the Personnel Department of Saint Bartholomew's Hospital, which, like all National Health hospitals, was run by managers and bureaucrats, rather than by consultants.

October had turned to mid-November and it was bitterly cold. The temperature was minus six and it was snowing heavily.

The Personnel Department at Saint Bartholomew's

110

Hospital was run by an extraordinary man who was only eighteen years old, and who was referred to by everyone as 'Mick the Rocker', because he always made nervous rock and roll movements whenever he spoke, even when he was sitting down. The words, 'Mick the Rocker's off his rocker' were written on the wall with a black felt-tipped pen, in one of the hospital's lavatories.

Mick the Rocker had a strong Yorkshire accent and struck those listening to him as being singular because of his persistent failure to use the definite article whenever he spoke.

It was a Friday afternoon at ten to five, a time when all Mick's staff were keen to get away for the weekend. He gathered his staff members together and called for a meeting to be held in the great hall of Saint Bartholomew's Hospital. In the great hall was a large, polished oak table with a jug of water and glasses for every staff member sitting at it. Jessie was called upon to take the minutes of the meeting although she was unable to take shorthand.

Mick continued to make nervous rock and roll movements and invited his staff members to sit down. He sat down as well. He began to speak and caused his audience to collapse in helpless giggles because of his nervous rock and roll movements and his failure to use the definite article, despite his high rank.

'There's an awful lot of necrophilia going on in mortry.* I know it's bloomin' rude but it's a soobject that's got to be addressed,' he began, still making nervous rock and roll movements.

* Mortuary

Mick the Rocker kept his staff members in the great hall of Saint Bartholomew's Hospital from ten to five until quarter past seven, repeating himself over and over again.

At least, Jessie was able to take down the minutes successfully and managed to make enough money to finance her next fix of heroin.

The next hospital Jessie was sent to was the Royal Free in Hampstead. She was sent there a week later. She was told to report to Personnel before going to the Psychiatric Department, on a Monday morning. She arrived over two hours late because her agency had not rung her up until eleven a.m.

Few of the offices in the Royal Free had natural light and the hospital's grossly overheated corridors occasionally echoed the screams of patients in pain. The depression that Jessie was suffering while she was on her way to the Personnel Manager's office was indescribable. The only thought preventing her from going home and hanging herself was that of her pregnancy with Lowther's baby which was in its early stages.

Pandora Duckett-Hamisley, a Wing-Commander's daughter, was a thirty-six-year-old Sloane Ranger. She had a strong public school accent, and was a vain, petulant, spoiled woman whose father had given her a dappled mare for her twenty-first birthday. She was not intelligent and had gained her position as Personnel Manager by starting off as an agency temp. She was pretty in a loud, Dallassy sort of way, with shoulder-length tinted blonde hair, cut in layers, a tailored navy blue suit and a strange, gaping grin.

Jessie was wearing the only formal outfit which she possessed. She had on a recently washed pink mini dress, a clean white cardigan, tanned tights and white patent boots to match her cardigan. On top of these clothes, she was wearing a white mink coat which she had stolen from a ladies' cloakroom. Her long black hair was coiled demurely on top of her head.

'My name's Jessie Lowther. I'm from the Medical and General Agency. I've come to fill the booking in the Psychiatric Department,' she said mechanically.

Pandora continued to grin inanely as if she were about to open a fête.

'We always double-book our temps to ensure that we're not let down. I've engaged another person besides you, so the booking has in fact been filled. I'm sure you'll understand,' she said, still smiling halfwittedly.

'So you've given instructions for me to come here without so much as an apology?' said Jessie angrily, adding, 'I've come all the way from Fulham.'

'I'm not here to take your inconvenience into consideration,' said Pandora, still smiling. Jessie lost her temper.

'Was that oafish grin sewn onto your face by a fucking plastic surgeon?' she shouted.

Pandora hadn't anticipated anything like this.

'Agency staff are frequently inefficient and unreliable. In addition, you are unacceptably rude. If you don't leave immediately, I shall call the porters and ask them to *throw* you out.'

'Not a chance, sister! You've got me round your neck

till you croak. Would you say something like that to a taxi-driver?'

'No, of course not, would you kindly...'

'I'm sure you wouldn't. Would you like to know why you wouldn't?'

Pandora was terrified of Jessie because she thought she was mad.

'Yes, all right,' she whispered.

'I'll tell you why. A taxi-driver would slit your throat. So would I if I had a knife.'

Jessie hurriedly left Pandora's office. She was not satisfied with being dismissed. She walked down the long corridor towards the Psychiatric Department of which Sally Lightman was the manager. Jessie had to ask about three people where the Psychiatric Department was. Sally had unmanageable, frizzy brown hair, scraped back from her face and a Croydon accent. She was not wearing any make-up and her skin was oily. She introduced herself to Jessie and told her how relieved she was that someone had turned up after such a long wait.

'I was told that this booking had already been filled,' said Jessie casually.

'No, that's not the case at all. I've been waiting for a secretary for a good two hours. Who gave you that information?'

'Oh, just someone I met in passing.'

Sally showed Jessie to her office which was dingy and damp and which looked on to a brick wall. The heat had been turned up ridiculously high. It was stifling. Sally told

Jessie that she would sign her time sheet on Friday afternoon at the close of business.

'You will be doing Dr Hogan's work,' said Sally. 'He sees patients in the room next door. Some of them are very noisy and aggressive. That's why it's so difficult to keep staff.'

Dr Greg Hogan came from Southern Australia although he had shed his Australian accent and spoke the Queen's English. He was softly spoken and was almost offensively nondescript. The only outstanding things about him were his marked lisp (similar to Jessie's), his strange high-pitched voice and his inability to pronounce his Rs. Also, he was extremely repetitive. He described almost every individual he met as being 'such a nice person', whether these people were nice or not.

He was a trendy left-winger whose wife, Jennifer, an ex-model, wore designer dresses and spent her spare time sending parcels containing food and drink to the women of Greenham Common. (These women were fanatical opponents of nuclear armament and seldom washed.)

Hogan enjoyed lucrative supplements to his salary by seeing private patients in Harley Street and was regarded by other members of the medical profession as being a 'lounge lizard Che Guevara'. He also irritated other consultants by borrowing their rooms in Harley Street because he was too stingy to rent them.

As if to compensate for his nondescript personality, Hogan drove an obscene-looking turquoise Citroën 2CV, its windscreen plastered with copious messages to traffic wardens in a flowing italic hand. He often parked it in Harley Street. On this particular occasion, he left this heinous heap of flashing, sky-blue metal in the Royal Free's car park and walked to his office.

One of his schizophrenic patients had built a miniature railway station which stretched from one side of the reception area of the Psychiatric Department to the other. Hogan tripped over it and fell flat on his face.

'Are you all right, Dr Hogan?' asked Sally.

Hogan got up.

'Yes, certainly. Of course I'm all right. It must have been Benjamin, the schizophrenic, who built the station. He's such a nice person.'

'We've found you a typist, Dr Hogan. It hasn't been easy to find staff since Suzie left. One doesn't really appreciate someone until after they've gone,' said Sally.

Hogan ran his hand through his thin, mouse-coloured hair.

'Yes, yes, of course. Of that there is no doubt at all. Suzie was such a nice person.'

Jessie introduced herself to Hogan.

'There's a discharge summary on Mrs Abigail Prendleblast to be done as a matter of urgency,' said Hogan. He turned to Sally. 'She's the lady who is wracked with embarrassment about her name, but she's such a nice person,' he added. He then turned to Jessie. 'You will find the tape on your desk. I'd like you to take one top and two carbons, one carbon to go in Mrs Prendleblast's casenotes and one to go in the discharge summary file. Sally will show you where that is. The patients' names must be in strict alphabetical order. After I've seen my next patient, I will call you in and give you some further dictation.'

'Miss Frances Wilberforce has just rung up to say that she will be ten minutes late,' said Sally. 'I do hope she won't make too much noise. She was shouting her head off on the phone.'

'I'm sure she won't cause any trouble,' said Hogan quietly. 'I've had a long letter from her GP. She sounds such a nice person.'

Miss Wilberforce was in her thirties. She had a loud, deep husky voice and a thick American accent of the Deep South, although she had become a British citizen. She was wearing a black, woollen sweater under a red pinafore dress and her crudely dyed black hair was parted in the centre and tied back in a ponytail. She had dyed it black, in order to match all her sweaters which were also black. She was noisy, agitated and nervy. She went up to Jessie who had started to type the discharge summary on Abigail Prendleblast.

'Where the hell's my psychiatrist?' demanded Miss Wilberforce.

'He's in the room next door. He's waiting for you there,' said Jessie, her tone of voice tense, due to her need for heroin.

The door between Jessie's office and Hogan's consulting room had been left ajar and she could hear everything that he and his patient were saying. The notion that this woman might possibly be just as disturbed and tortured as she was comforted her a little.

Miss Wilberforce was drunk when she entered the consulting room. She staggered towards Hogan's chair and fell over. She was carrying a bottle of gin in her bag, and added to this with a couple of swigs.

'What can I do for you?' asked Hogan quietly. (He failed to rise to his feet. His patient found this rather rude but failed to say so.)

Miss Wilberforce looked suspiciously round the room. Her bright hazel eyes focused for some time on the chairs in front of Hogan's desk. She looked dissatisfied.

'Where the hell's your couch?' she barked.

'My couch?' exclaimed Hogan.

'Yes. You heard very well what I said. A psychiatrist without a couch is like a gravedigger without a spade. This is a singularly unsatisfactory state of affairs.'

In an adjoining room was a bunk with its lower bed missing. It would not have been possible to get up onto it without a ladder. Miss Wilberforce went into the other room.

'Why haven't you got a ladder?' she asked aggressively.

Hogan straightened his tie nervously.

'If you are really adamant that you would like to lie down, I will help you up.'

'It looks as if you're going to have to. Kneel on the floor.'

Hogan did as he was told. He lived in a permanent village idiot's euphoria and enjoyed being abused by women, but his enjoyment never equalled the thrill which he experienced when he was being ordered about by bureaucratic personnel managers and hospital administrators.

The top level of the bunk was so high that Miss Wilberforce couldn't see Hogan's head from where she was lying.

'I can't see your head from where I am lying. Again, I find this singularly unsatisfactory. You will have to stand on a chair.'

Hogan picked up a chair and put it close to the bunk. Then he stood on it. He did not have a sufficient sense of humour to find the situation comical.

'What can I do for you?' he repeated quietly.

'You are standing too close to me. Go and stand in the other room.'

Hogan obeyed and once more he asked her what he could do for her.

It was clear that Miss Wilberforce was mentally disturbed but her suffering appeared in no way equal to Jessie's and the more she (Jessie) listened to the consultation, the more desolate and lonely she became.

'Have you had any experiences with psychiatrists before?' asked Hogan gently.

'Yeah, I've seen shrinks before,' said Miss Wilberforce, her husky voice raised to a resonant boom. 'The last arsehole I saw told me I had paranoid schizophrenia, just because I lay down on his couch, forgetting to take off my overcoat, scarf and gloves. It was midsummer but that's neither here nor there,' she added.

Hogan looked at her aghast. As he watched his patient, her glittering hazel eyes stared vacantly into space, showing neither rage nor emotional disturbance.

'Why have you come to see me?' he asked.

Miss Wilberforce produced a flick-knife with a three-inch blade and flicked it open and shut. This distressed Jessie because it reminded her of Mark Oppenheimer, who had long since committed suicide, and of a period in her life before she had embarked on heroin.

A long silence ensued.

Click H-whitt. Click H-whitt. Click H-whitt. Click H-whitt.

The silence was broken by Hogan's terrified, high-pitched voice.

'Would you put your flick-knife away, please, Miss Wilberforce. Psychiatrists have rights.'

'That's just where you're wrong, my bucko. Psychiatrists haven't got any goddamned rights. They are there to be spat at and abused.'

'Why have you come to see me if you've got no respect for my profession?'

'Psychiatrists have abused me all my life. A psychiatrist is his patient's cur. You are all beneath contempt. You ought to be garrotted with piano wire, the whole lousy lot of you.'

'Then how do you imagine I can possibly help you?'

'Because no one else can. I've got a dreadful habit in which I feel it is my duty to indulge and which I can't stop.'

'Tell me about it,' said Hogan calmly.

'Someone I worship owns a national newspaper. I will not give his name at this stage. I adore him because he saved my life when I was in my teens. Every night, I drive my Ferrari to his rival's newspaper's building and I go into the machine room where I throw umbrellas and cooking utensils into the presses so that his rival's newspapers come out with blank front pages. I hang about with a bag of nails on the passenger's seat of my Ferrari. As soon as my friend's rival's newspaper's lorries leave to distribute their first editions, I grab a fistful of nails and pull out. I crush the nails into the palm of my hand until my skin bleeds and I throw them out of the window on the driver's side of my Ferrari in front of the lorries travelling behind me. As I drive the nails into my flesh, I sing,' (Miss Wilberforce broke into song), ' "*We plough the fields and scatter the good seed on the land…*" and I experience an extraordinary sensation of joy.'

'Who is this newspaper proprietor? What is his name? What newspaper does he own?' ventured Hogan.

Miss Wilberforce smiled shiftily. 'As a matter of fact, his name is Sir Jasper Montrose. He is universally known. He owns *The Fleet Street Herald*. His rival, and arch enemy, is Ted Morris who owns *The Fleet Street Times*,' said Miss Wilberforce in a reverent tone of voice.

'How did Sir Jasper Montrose save your life when you were in your teens?' asked Hogan.

'Oh, I was binned by two crooked shrinks. In other words, I was bunged into a fucking lunatic asylum. I had a ghastly time in there. Sir Jasper came to me one morning and simply took me by the hand, led me out of the loony bin and asked his driver to take me to his house. I admit he is a highly controversial person in that he is a wealthy socialist, and some sons of a bitches call him a crook, but I adore him and have had a very loving relationship with him, ever since he rescued me. I won't hear a fucking word against him.'

'If you've got such a loving relationship with him, he must be such a nice person,' said Hogan tactfully.

Miss Wilberforce smiled.

'Hey, you're not such a schmuck after all,' she exclaimed. 'You're about the only shrink I've met who doesn't deserve to be garrotted with piano wire.'

Hogan nervously straightened his tie. 'I take that as a backhanded compliment,' he eventually managed to mutter. 'Do you ever get an orgasm when you throw out the nails?' he added.

'Sure thing, man.'

Hogan cleared his throat.

'You are, I take it, aware that your actions are strictly illegal?' he commented mildly.

'I am aware that they are but I still can't control them.'

'Does Sir Jasper Montrose know what you are doing?'

'No!' shouted Miss Wilberforce. There was a hysterical tone of horror in her voice.

Another silence ensued. Jessie wondered whether Marcia's father knew Sir Jasper Montrose. There was much in Miss Wilberforce which reminded Jessie of Marcia, who was a member of a newspaper family and whom she had so deeply hurt. Her despair and accompanying guilt intensified.

'Would you come in, please?' said Hogan to Jessie after Miss Wilberforce had left. 'I want you to type a letter to Miss Wilberforce's GP. Let me know if I dictate too fast. Do you take shorthand?'

'I'm afraid not,' confessed Jessie.

'That's all right,' said Hogan kindly, adding, 'I will dictate very slowly. I want you to type a letter to Miss Wilberforce's GP,' he repeated.

Dear Dr Upton,
Thank you for referring a really fascinating patient. She came to me already drunk with her speech somewhat slurred. She had a bottle of gin in her bag and added to this with a couple of swigs. I agree she is highly schizoid although I have not seen enough of her to reach a diagnostic conclusion. It is likely, after subsequent discussions with her, that I will arrive at an unequivocal diagnosis of schizophrenia.
On examination, I was struck by her deliberate and slow manner of speech. Today, she behaved just as bizarrely as she did on the phone and insisted on lying down in another room, as far away from me as possible, and talking to me through an open door.
In addition, she toyed with a flick-knife throughout the consultation and asked me to stand on a chair...

Pandora, the Personnel Manager, stormed into Hogan's consulting room, looking irate and flustered. She failed to knock on the door.

'Excuse me, Dr Hogan. I have already asked your secretary to leave,' she said, her voice raised.

'What's all this about?' asked Hogan quietly.

'I don't feel that this woman is suitable to fill this booking. She threatened to slit my throat,' said Pandora.

'I beg your pardon?'

'She is foul-tempered and undesirable. I want her to leave now.'

'That's all very well but have you got a replacement?'

'I don't know yet. Mrs Lowther, please get your things together and leave the premises,' said Pandora.

'But she has already taken down a letter for me,' said Hogan. 'Do let her finish typing it back first.'

'That is out of the question. I hope I will not have to repeat myself,' said Pandora arrogantly.

'Very well,' said Hogan, adding, 'even so, she strikes me as being such a nice person.'

'You might have to go without a secretary for a day or two. This woman is totally unsuitable, as I said.'

Jessie came into the room, violently kicking open the door which knocked over a framed photograph of Hogan's wife, Jennifer, wearing one of her designer dresses.

'This woman said she'd double-booked and that the booking had been filled by another secretary, so she's lying,' shouted Jessie. 'Come on, Dr Hogan, you're a consultant, for God's sake! You can't allow a jumped-up personnel manager to rule your life,' she added.

'Hospitals are run by administrators and personnel managers, not consultants,' said Hogan, his voice scarcely above a whisper.

'Oh? And can some cheap bureaucrat tell you what secretary to appoint?'

Hogan lowered his head in embarrassment. 'Well, these are the rules and that is how the National Health Service is run,' he muttered after a pause.

'What, by lying bitches like her?'

Pandora had already called the porters to remove Jessie by force. She was in desperate need of heroin, without having enough money to buy it, and she was carried out of the hospital kicking and screaming.

'I've got news for you, Dr Hogan. Once you're dead and buried, no one will know or care that you ever existed,' shouted Jessie as she was being carried out of the office by the totally baffled porters.

Even if she had been paid for a day's work, Jessie would only have been able to afford enough heroin for one injection. She walked all the way from Hampstead to Shepherd's Market, off Park Lane, through the wind and sleet of the freezing November afternoon.

She intended to sell her body in order to finance her next fix. She uncoiled her black hair and let it flow to her waist.

She stood on the pavement between two prostitutes, both of whom were smoking. One of them was wearing a clinging black rubber suit, thigh-high stiletto snakeskin boots and an Arctic fox shawl. Her name was Sharon Taylor but she was known to some of her clients as 'Mademoiselle Wagon Lit,' because she commuted to London almost every day from Milton Keynes and paid her fare by picking up punters on the train and having sex with them in the lavatory.

Sharon came from an impoverished background and a broken home. Her father was an out-of-work drunk who beat his wife and daughter up on occasions when he was sober enough to stand. Sharon and her mother were the family breadwinners. Her mother was an ageing hooker who, like her daughter, touted for trade on the train from Milton Keynes to London.

The other prostitute was called Samantha Clarke. She was wearing a short, white leather miniskirt and was bare-breasted beneath a tight yellow sweater. She had on a pair of white stiletto heeled shoes and her legs were bare and purple in the icy wind, and covered with weeping red scars. There was a bloodstained bandage under her left knee which reminded Jessie of a painting by Hieronymus Bosch. Despite the cold weather, she wasn't wearing an overcoat.

Jessie's shivers, blocked sinuses, dry, scratchy throat and aching stomach took her mind off the vicious melancholia which had eaten into her brain since her father had been shot on the Austrian border. Her stomach pain had deteriorated from a dull ache to an agony so intense that she might as well have had a carving knife in her guts with its handle rotating. She fell to her knees and was sick in the gutter. Somehow, prostitutes can tell if another prostitute uses heroin.

Mademoiselle Wagon Lit didn't give Jessie a chance to finish being sick. She grabbed hold of her hair and jerked her head backwards, causing her to be sick on her clothes.

'Piss off, will yer!' she shouted. 'We don't want no bloomin' junkies on our beat, screwing up our trade.'

Jessie had no will to fight any more. She knelt in the gutter and yearned for death to come quickly. The other prostitute turned on her as well. The two women dragged her away from Shepherd's Market until they all reached

Park Lane. Jessie's skin was itching so much that she clawed at her face. Somehow, she managed to clean away the vomit on her clothes.

Whatever could be said about her appearance that afternoon, she had redeemingly good legs enhanced by her patent white boots and golden brown tights which made her legs look suntanned. Also, her stolen mink coat looked extremely smart, as did her waist-length black hair which blew behind her in the savage wind.

* * *

Brigadier Plato Poynings had been labelled by tabloid gossip columnists as being the most eccentric man in Britain. His mother had divorced her army officer husband, due to his persistent womanizing, when Plato was eighteen months old. She remarried an Arab Sheik who paid for her son's education at Harrow.* Although Halil Al Hassan, the Arab Sheik, was not his real father, Plato worshipped him and clung in a doting, blinkered way to the Muslim beliefs which he had imposed on him while he sat on his knee. After his death, Plato remembered him for his ear to ear grin and flashing gold teeth.

Brigadier Plato Poynings read a section from the Koran every morning before he went to his office. He was an architect and had been commissioned to design the mausoleum of King Hussein of Jordan.† Poynings had an uncommonly distinguished face and a black goatee beard.

*A boy's public school.
†King Hussein of Jordan was born on the fourteenth of November, nineteen thirty-five and he died on the seventh of February, nineteen ninety-nine.

He worked on his plans and drawings from ten o'clock in the morning till noon when he had a meal consisting of smoked salmon, toast, caviar and vodka. He consumed a large amount of liquor every day, contrary to his Muslim beliefs. He spent most of the afternoons drinking in the Wig and Pen, a pub which was patronized by wealthy drunks. He sometimes met other architects there and liked to discuss shop with them. He worked on his plans for part of the afternoons as well. At about four o'clock in the afternoon, he habitually travelled in the back of his chauffeur-driven Rolls-Royce, picking up loose women.

On that cold, frosty November afternoon, his chauffeur was driving him down Park Lane. Poynings was looking at his drawings of King Hussein's mausoleum. He was feeling cheerful and jolly and held up massive sheets of paper in front of him (namely sheets of paper regarding the design of King Hussein's tomb), blocking the driver's mirror, talking and chuckling to himself out loud.

'No, no, Poynings dear. The catafalque area should be in white marble in keeping with the rest of the vault. The idea that each vault should be within a greater vault is out, out, out in designing mausoleums for the great and noble. Really, Poynings, this isn't Egypt, you know. The whole mausoleum should be kept as simple as possible.'

'Did you say something, sir?' asked his chauffeur.

'No, no, Jones, oh, no, no, no and sons limited. I was talking to myself.'

'Do you think you could please stop stretching out those

large sheets of paper? I can't see a thing through the rear mirror, sir,' ventured Jones.

'What's wrong with the wing mirror?' asked Poynings with a rasp in his voice.

Jones was being paid the same wage as a Harley Street surgeon and could be sacked at a moment's notice.

'I apologize, sir. It was extremely remiss of me,' he muttered.

'Oh, Jones?'

'Sir?'

'That girl out there with the waist length jet-black hair blowing in the wind and the wonderfully shapely, sun-tanned legs?'

'What about her, sir?'

'Why does she keep falling over, clutching her stomach?'

'I've got no idea. Menstrual pains, perhaps, begging your pardon, sir.'

'Don't be disgusting, Jones. Pull into the side, this instant.'

'Very good, sir.'

Poynings leant out of the window and called to Jessie.

'My dear lady.'

'I know how to give a man a good time, I do,' shouted Jessie coarsely.

'Come on Jones, I told you to pull in, you damned fool.'

'Very good, sir.' Jones pulled into the side of the road.

Poynings reached out of the window of his Rolls-Royce, clutched Jessie's hand and sang, '*My Love is like a Red, Red Rose.*'

'It's no good your just sitting there, singing your bloody

head off! Are you going to fuck me or aren't you?' said Jessie vulgarly.

Poynings got out of the Rolls, carrying a plastic bag in which he kept a cassette recorder and a jar of Vaseline.

'I'm going to my suite in the Dortch,* Jones. Come and collect me in about an hour's time.'

'Very good, sir.'

Jones suddenly got out of the Rolls and followed his boss.

'Oh, sir?'

'Yes. What the devil do you want, Jones?'

'Have you remembered your rubbers?'†

'Confound your damnable impertinence, Jones! Forfeit one hundred pounds from this week's wages.'

'Very good, sir. I apologize, sir.'

The saucy *Sun* didn't call Brigadier Poynings 'Potty Plato' for nothing. He was kinky. He liked prostitutes of each sex to push wooden objects up his behind while he listened to a rousing Russian folk song called *Kasbek* (a song which started slowly and gradually gathered speed), and a zippy but phenomenally haunting tune called 'Red Partisans' from the film, *Doctor Zhivago*.

Jessie obliged him by using his walking stick, which she had been told to dip into Poynings's jar of Vaseline first.

He was satisfied with her work. He gave her a hundred pounds. It never crossed his mind that she was a heroin addict and he thought that she had no more than a chill and a fever. She told him that she was available for two

* Dorchester Hotel.
† Condoms.

130

days a week and he offered her secretarial work to start when she got better. She reasoned that non-medical secretarial work was better than nothing.

Jessie went straight to her dealer, an out-of-work West Indian called Cuthbert Scantlebury who lived in a small council flat off the Earls Court Road. Scantlebury was a drug addict himself and dealt in heroin in order to support his habit. (He charged fifty pounds for each dose of heroin.)

When Jessie had had her injection in a public lavatory, she went home to Lowther, relieved to be free from the cramps in her stomach, but she was still tormented by the melancholia which even the heroin couldn't lift any more. She had always felt comforted by Lowther's love. She mounted the stairs two at a time and held the loose, creaking banisters to quicken her ascent.

Animated conversation and peals of laughter were coming from the room which Jessie shared with Lowther. Jessie waited outside and listened. She heard the voices of two men. One of them was Lowther's and his Edinburgh accent was more pronounced than usual. The other man, Liam Hennessy, had a thick southern Irish accent and a voice much louder than Lowther's. Hennessy had embarked on a rambling monologue.

'You should have seen the bugger who picked me up last night. He was a Brit. He was dressed from head to foot in fucking black leather, and he just banged on and on in his typically British way about him being the master and me being the bloody servant. He was such a bore.'

Jessie could hear Lowther's delighted laughter.

'Not only was he a bore. He was dead selfish and inconsiderate. All through the night, he did all the pitchin' and he made me do all the catchin',' continued Hennessy.

Jessie was suddenly reminded of the story which Marcia had written at school about the two Red Army soldiers, and although she hated the place, she felt a pang of nostalgia, as well as guilt about her treatment of Marcia.

'He was awful,' Hennessy went on. 'I don't know what was the most offensive thing about him, the fact that he had on these crude leopard-skin printed knickers or the fact that he hadn't even heard of the legendary Patrick Pearse.'*

Jessie kicked open the door and went straight in. She had never for one moment expected to find the two men in bed. She had no idea that her husband was bisexual. Lowther was naked. He scrambled out of bed and covered himself with a filthy towel.

'You've been gone for so long, I thought you'd walked out on me,' he muttered.

Jessie stared at the two men in disbelief. Then she pulled a pair of blue jeans, a thick, navy blue polo-necked sweater, a shabby black leather jacket, a pair of training shoes and a pair of socks from a cupboard and pushed them into a plastic bag, before shouting the words, 'I'm divorcing you! I can't stand brown-hatters.'† She went downstairs and got into Lowther's battered old black Ford Estate which he

---

*Notorious Irish rebel. He was tried by court-martial and executed by a firing squad in Kilmainham Jail on the third of May nineteen-sixteen.

†The slang term 'brown-hatters', which is extremely vulgar, is frequently used to describe homosexuals. It has a phallic connection. The author refrains from defining this expression, other than to say that it is self-explanatory.

had forgotten to lock. She remembered how she had reacted when she found Digby Taylor's body hanging in the barn. She told herself that what she had witnessed was only a hallucination.

She lived in the Ford for the next few days and used it as a mobile home. This mode of living reminded her of the days when she had travelled round western Hungary with her father and she experienced a warped sense of stability. Every night, she lay down in the back of the car, using a pile of music sheets as a pillow. She also turned the engine on, thus enabling her to heat the car which had recently been filled with petrol. She worked for Poynings for two days a week and finally decided to return to the Royal Academy of Music.

A brief letter from Keith Johnson, the Director of the Royal Academy of Music, awaited her in her mailbox.

Dear Mrs Lowther,

As the Director of the Royal Academy of Music, I have reached the conclusion that your prolonged absences from the Academy, unqualified by medical certificates, are unacceptable.

You have chosen to ignore two written warnings. This behaviour is incompatible with the regulations of the Academy and I am regrettably faced with no choice but to ask you to abandon your studies here.

Yours sincerely,

Keith Johnson

Director of the Royal Academy of Music (Dictated by Mr Johnson and sent in his absence)

The letter had a numbing effect on Jessie. She realized that she had lost her chance of becoming an internationally famous musician. This, combined with Lowther's bisexuality, was dreadful enough in itself and it wouldn't have been possible for her to feel more suicidal than she did then.

Poynings had a young clerk working for him called Alan Winterbottom. He was a heavily-built, coarse-featured man with a loud voice and a cockney accent. He looked like a man who spent much of his spare time singing obscene songs in rugger players' changing-rooms. He invited Jessie out for a drink after work one evening. Winterbottom had once been a heroin addict but he had weaned himself off the drug. He was an extravagant gambler and was unable to live off his salary alone. He sold heroin in order to supplement his modest income and lived in a small, dirty flat in Bethnal Green in London's East End.

'Why did you ask me to come out for a drink with you?' asked Jessie suspiciously.

'You use smack, don't you? I can always tell,' said Winterbottom.

'What's it to you if I do?'

'I was on it once. Now I sell it.'

'I've already got a pusher. He charges me fifty pounds for each fix,' said Jessie.

'Why not switch to me? I only charge a pony.'

'What the hell do you mean by "a pony"?' asked Jessie rudely.

'You don't know much, do you? It means twenty-five quid.'

Jessie accompanied Winterbottom to the filthy flat in which he lived. He sold her some white powder in tin foil. She went to Lowther's Ford to inject herself by pouring the white powder with water into a dessert spoon, and heating the spoon from underneath it with a cigarette lighter. The powder was a mixture of talcum powder, flour and sand with only ten per cent of heroin added. If a well-wishing woman hadn't called for help when she saw Jessie lying on her back in an East End of London backstreet with her lips black and her face ashen, she would have died.

An ambulance was called. So were the police. Jessie was admitted to hospital for a week. The police found stored sachets of heroin in the boot of the Ford which she had been living in. She had hoarded these in case of an emergency. The heroin had been paid for by cash stolen from the till in Poynings's offices. She was charged with theft and was accused (unfairly) of selling heroin to enable her to buy it. She was jailed for nine months.

She shared a cell with a blackmailer and a child molester. She was unable to inject herself with heroin for obvious reasons. She chilled out and her withdrawal symptoms were horrific for her, and downright terrifying for her two companions. It required at least seven people to hold Jessie down during the initial withdrawal. Her two cell-mates were two of the luckless seven. The remainder were five prison officers. The suffering that Jessie had to undergo was three times as bad as a really bad attack of flu.

During the first two months of her sentence, Jessie tried to commit suicide by hanging herself in her cell, after tying her sheets together and making a noose out of them. As her sentence progressed, however, so did her pregnancy with Lowther's baby. Her yearning for a blood relation gave her strength. She gave birth to a boy in the prison hospital and she called him Zoltan after one of her criminal ancestors. He inherited his mother's and his grandfather's large grey eyes and jet-black hair.

Once she was released from prison on a cold January morning, she had another stroke of luck. Jeanette's mother, Jean, had just died, and as she and her daughter did not get on, Jean left five hundred thousand pounds to Jessie who was able to buy a caravan and a brand new Land Rover to tow it. She was also able to put an upright piano, a harp, as well as a guitar in the caravan and planned to travel all over the country in it, taking Zoltan with her, just as her father had taken her.

There was no one to look after Zoltan so she carried him on her back everywhere she went. There was a film which she wanted to see at the Odeon Haymarket. She walked past Poynings's offices nearby and was about to cross the road when Winterbottom bumped into her. It was still January and he was wearing a thick jacket under a fur-lined overcoat.

'Where have you been all this time, Jessie?' he asked.

'Prison,' she replied acidly. 'You gave me a lethal dose of mixed up smack.'

'Don't take it so badly. I had no idea it was mixed up when I bought it. It wasn't my fault.

'Nothing's ever your fault!' shouted Jessie.

'Please don't take it like that. A friend of mine is giving a fancy dress party on Saturday night, in his basement flat, at number ten, Dewhurst Road, Hammersmith. I'm going as Hitler. Would you like to come?'

'Yes, I'll come.'

'Good. What will you come as?'

'Just as I was. A junkie, even though I'm clean now,' said Jessie in a surly tone of voice.

Jessie went to the Hammersmith basement flat in Dewhurst Road with Zoltan strapped to her back and left him with a kindly old lady who said she would look after him in her flat on the ground floor of the building. Jessie's only motive for going to the fancy dress party was loneliness. A young woman at the party was weepy and drunk. She had come as Elizabeth the First. She was quarrelling bitterly with a man who had been two-timing her and who was dressed as Sir Walter Raleigh. Winterbottom strode into the room dressed as Hitler, brandishing a riding whip. He had smoked a lot of cannabis before arriving at the flat in Dewhurst Road. His mounting debts had increased. He sat down and decided to get systematically drunk, having told everyone in the room that he was heavily in debt.

Jessie had a burning desire to take her revenge on Winterbottom. A wicked idea festered within her.

'Where did you get your uniform from, Alan?' she asked casually.

'Sainsbury's,' replied Winterbottom, which confirmed Jessie's suspicions that he was very drunk indeed, as well as being proverbially stupid.

Jessie took him gently by the hand and led him out into the corridor. He was puzzled by her seemingly forgiving gesture.

'I heard you saying that you were in debt,' she remarked.

'That's right. I'm in terrible debt. Times ain't easy.'

'I'm so sorry to hear that. I've got an idea. I know a very rich man in Kensington called Mr Lenin. He's a homosexual pervert with a *penchant* for burly men in Nazi uniforms. He likes them to break into his house and spit in front of his portrait on the wall in the small hours of the morning. He will pay a thousand pounds in cash to anyone prepared to do this.'

'What does he look like?' asked Winterbottom.

'His portrait won't be hard to find. He's a bald-headed, nondescript looking man, wearing a waistcoat, tie and jacket. He will lean over the banisters and watch you spitting in front of his portrait and, if he is satisfied with your performance, he will throw the money down to you in fifty pound notes. Then he will come downstairs and ask you to perform fellatio on him.'

'You mean – suck his cock?'

'You're on to it,' said Jessie assertively.

'Who is this man?' asked Winterbottom, his speech slurred.

'He's no one well-known but he's one of the richest men in London and he's also very generous. He's inherited about two million pounds from his late father. If he likes your performance, he will throw down a thousand pounds in fifty pound notes, as I said,' replied Jessie.

'How do you know all this?' asked Winterbottom.

'I read about it in *Private Eye*.'

'What's that?'

'It's a satirical magazine, you ignoramus. It comes out once a fortnight.'

Winterbottom was so drunk and stoned that he found Jessie's words acceptable. It was almost two o'clock in the morning. He staggered into Jessie's Land Rover carrying his whip. Jessie drove fast, spurred on by a burning desire for revenge and a festering, livid hatred for the man who had nearly killed her by selling her impure heroin. She thought nothing of the fact that she had not passed her driving test. She knew vaguely how to drive as Lowther had given her a few driving lessons in his Ford. She had also had about twenty lessons from the British School of Motoring.

She drove her Land Rover from Hyde Park Corner to Knightsbridge and into Kensington Gore. From there, she swerved into Kensington Park Gardens. A sentry sprang from his box and tried to stop her but she was coming straight at him. He jumped out of her way.

Jessie remembered where the Soviet Embassy was from the day when she went there with Marcia. She screeched to a halt outside the Embassy. Winterbottom had slumped over the dash.

'You're not going to be sick are you?' Jessie asked anxiously.

'No,' replied Winterbottom. He didn't sound convincing.

He then raised his head and stared at the Soviet flag which fluttered and flapped in the biting January wind.

'What's that red thing?' he asked inanely.

'Do you mean that piece of red cloth? That's Mr Lenin's bath towel. He's put it out to dry, despite the cold. If you're wondering about the yellow insignia in the corner, that's his family crest. His ancestors were carpenters and farmers. The hammer represents the carpenters and the sickle represents the farmers.'

Winterbottom was satisfied.

'Just climb over the gate and bang peremptorily on the door,' said Jessie, adding, 'it's very important to be really rude and aggressive. You will probably find a rather sleepy-looking man just inside the door. He's Mr Lenin's servant. Don't worry about him. All you have to do is push him roughly aside. That's all part of the turn on, like the rudeness and the aggression. Just say, "I've come to spit in front of the portrait of Lenin on the wall, and suck his cock afterwards."'

'Are you sure Mr Lenin will be there?'

'Most definitely. One of my friends made a thousand pounds from him only the other night.'

Winterbottom got out of Jessie's Land Rover and took his riding whip with him. He climbed up the iron gate leading to the Soviet Embassy, but his clothing somehow got caught on top of the gate. His cap fell to the frosty ground on the other side of the gate, onto Soviet soil.

Winterbottom tried to get over to the other side but he couldn't get his clothing off the top of the gate. His bladder was full. He was terrified of emptying it before he'd accomplished his task. Unbeknown to him, a police car had pulled up outside the Soviet Embassy. Winterbottom lost his temper and started shouting.

'Is there a dickhead in there called Lenin?'

Lights were switched on in the embassy. Winterbottom thought that he would soon have an audience and his relief fuelled his rage.

'What the hell does this sodding shithead, Lenin, mean by asking me to come pissing all the way over here in this bloody cold weather, just to spit in front of his portrait and suck his fucking cock? I can tell you one thing, Mr Lenin. When I get into your house, I'm going to bugger you till your balls come out of your stinking arsehole!'

A policeman reached up and tapped Winterbottom on the leg.

'Excuse me, sir. What seems to be the trouble?'

'You've got no business interfering,' snarled Winterbottom. 'I'm trying to do my job.'

'Your job?' exclaimed the astonished policeman. 'Who are you? What do you think you're doing? This is the Soviet Embassy. Get down from there at once.'

Winterbottom cracked his whip over the policeman's head.

'Soviet Embassy? Soviet bloody Embassy? Don't start getting funny with me.'

'Get down from there this instant. What's your name?'

'My name is Trotsky and I'm Jessie's aunt,' replied Winterbottom who was still pie-eyed.

'I thought I told you to get down. This is my third time of asking!'

'Sir Winston Churchill wouldn't have stood for any of this fucking treatment, Officer,' screamed Winterbottom. (By this time he was hysterical.)

'Sir Winston Churchill,' bellowed the policeman, 'was not in the habit of breaking into Soviet Embassies in a Nazi uniform at two o'clock in the morning, using obscene language, cracking a riding whip and saying he was someone's aunt!'

Winterbottom fell to the ground outside the embassy gates like an India rubber ball, having torn his clothing. The policeman spoke into his radio.

'An aggressive, foul-mouthed man in a Nazi uniform has been trying to break into the Soviet Embassy, Sergeant.'

'You don't understand. A woman told me that a man called Lenin liked burly men in Nazi uniforms to spit in front of his portrait, and suck his cock afterwards.'

'I beg your pardon?'

'It's not my fault. This isn't fair. A woman put me up to it, as I said.'*

'Oh, she did, did she? I'm afraid I'm going to have to sling you down the nick. Do you realize that you could have triggered off a major international incident?'

Jessie got out of her Land Rover and stood behind Winterbottom.

'Oh, Officer, where is your sense of humour?' she exclaimed.

'If I were you, sir, I'd watch the kind of company you keep,' said the policeman.

*The author had a similar experience to this in April 1975. She disapproved of a man wearing a Nazi uniform at a fancy dress party, so she punished him by driving him to the Soviet Embassy. The man was very anti-Semitic and was a member of the National Front. The author drove a Mini Clubman Estate, not a Land Rover. She was only twenty-four years old at the time.

'Don't worry,' said Jessie. 'In future, I will. This evil bastard nearly killed me. He's a drug pusher. He sold me a sachet of junk with a small amount of heroin added, having implied that it was pure heroin. He sold it to me for a pony, in other words, twenty-five pounds. Mercifully, I'm clean now,' she added as an afterthought.

The policeman cleared his throat. He jumped up and down as he spoke, to protect himself from the cold.

'I see there will be quite a few things to discuss once I've taken you to the police station,' he said to Winterbottom.

Winterbottom's flat was searched and a large quantity of heroin mixed with talcum powder, flour and sand was found. After court hearings (first in a magistrates' court and finally in a Crown court), he was given a stiff custodial sentence for possession and sale of heroin mixed with talcum powder, flour and sand.

* * *

January turned to February and February to March. Spring had arrived early. Jessie had everything she could have wished for. She was now nationally famous and her fifth symphony in E flat major had recently been played on Radio Three under her original name. She had plenty of money, a caravan, a Land Rover to tow it with and the thing that she craved more than anything else in the world, a blood relation. However, her stupefying melancholia still had not lifted because its roots were so deeply embedded in her psyche.

The first thing Jessie needed was a driving licence to enable her to drive her Land Rover for long distances.

She thought she had had enough lessons to pass her test. She gained her licence illegally. During the test, she nervously skipped two red lights and failed to slow down at a zebra crossing when an old lady wanted to cross the road. The driving examiner crossed himself. 'Such a gesture I consider to be extremely impertinent,' said Jessie with uncharacteristic pomposity.

Eventually, the test was over. Jessie was wearing an extremely short red leather mini skirt in order to attract the examiner who said, 'That's the end of the test but I'm afraid you haven't passed.'

Jessie took five hundred pounds in fifty pound notes from her handbag and waved them ostentatiously in front of the examiner. She massaged his thigh and undid his zip.

'Five hundred pounds and a nice blow job say I *have* passed,' she said vulgarly. The examiner lost his head. He put the five hundred pounds into his wallet and allowed Jessie to perform fellatio on him until he ejaculated down her throat, and nearly choked her. Once she recovered her breath, the corrupt examiner gave her a pink slip, which indicated that she had passed her driving test. Jessie then successfully applied for a driving licence.

She and Zoltan travelled round England in the caravan, taking with them a golden Labrador puppy called 'Landy' which was short for 'Orlando'. They travelled aimlessly round England and Scotland for seven years. During that time, Jessie worked hard, writing music. She was able to disperse some of her melancholia by drinking a bottle of gin a day. It took her a few hours to travel west from

North East England to a desolate part of Wales, where she and Zoltan settled for a while. Jessie had found it too cold in North East England which was why she decided to move and Zoltan agreed with the move.

Jessie told Zoltan about his roguish, fearless ancestors. She also explained to him the Legend of the Zartak Knife. She told Zoltan that if the Zartak Knife were repossessed by one of Zartak blood, that person would know everlasting fame and joy. She gave Zoltan the oblong, wooden box which her father had given her and explained what was written on the parchment that it contained, namely greater details than those which she had already given him to describe the Legend.

Jessie failed to send Zoltan to school. She educated him to a certain extent herself. She taught him how to speak a smattering of Hungarian and also how to read and write music and play the piano. She did not teach him how to read and write words, however.

A certain Joe Murphy, who was a vindictive friend of Winterbottom's, had given the number of Jessie's Land Rover to the police. Somehow, Jessie managed to change the number plate. Murphy informed the police of Jessie's drink problem which he said was causing her to be cruel to Zoltan, and to deny him the education which was required by law. Because of the changed number plate and the fact that Jessie and her son rarely stayed in the same place for a long period of time, it took the plodding police several years to track the caravan down.

* * *

145

It was some time shortly after Christmas. Jessie had lost track of the date and the time. She and Zoltan both had severe bronchitis which never seemed to clear up. Zoltan had already had his seventh birthday. One morning there was a knock at the door of the caravan and Jessie knew that someone would one day take the only thing she loved away from her. She told her son to hide under the bed behind the screen in the corner of the caravan. (She and Zoltan shared the bed, which was narrow and unmade. There were no clean sheets – only a pile of filthy blankets.) Jessie came to the door wearing jeans, her navy blue polo-necked sweater, a shabby black leather jacket, filthy training shoes and unwashed socks – the clothes which she had taken from the wardrobe when she had walked out on Lowther. Her breath stank strongly of stale gin.

'Who are you and what do you want?' she demanded.

The woman she saw was wearing a drab, ill-fitting tweed suit, outmoded shoes and no make-up. She had a strong Welsh accent.

'I'm Gladys Evans. I'm a social worker.'

Jessie was seized by a fit of coughing. The more she coughed, the more she exhaled the stench of stale gin. Her eyes were swollen and bloodshot. It was obvious that she was pie-eyed, even at nine-thirty in the morning.

'I understand you've got a seven-year-old son. It is also evident that you've got a drink problem and it has been reported to the authorities that you have been ill-treating your son.'

Jessie called the social worker a battery of obscene names

146

and tried to throw her out of the caravan but Gladys rammed her foot in the door.

'What school does your son attend?' she demanded.

'My son, Zoltan, died of whooping cough aged eighteen months. Why else do you think I drink?' shouted Jessie.

Gladys looked puzzled.

'I find that hard to believe. He is on the Register of Births and was born on the second of August, nineteen —. He is not on the Register of Deaths which indicates that not only is he still alive, he is also seven years old. Where is he?'

Jessie uttered another battery of obscenities. She threw Gladys out of the caravan, dragging her by the hair. Throughout the next few weeks, more and more social workers descended on her, asking her where Zoltan was. Although the threat of losing him was becoming increasingly real, Jessie gradually became immune to the social workers' visits.

She realized that her only hope of keeping Zoltan with her would be to leave Wales and travel somewhere else but she also knew that a bottle of gin in her system every day, combined with her high fever, would affect her driving and put her son's life at risk.

'Will those nasty women be coming back again?' asked Zoltan. He had just played *Für Elise* for Jessie on the piano. He had played the piece beautifully, including the complex part in the middle.

Jessie hugged her son and wept piteously. It would only have taken the law to declare her unfit to be a mother to destroy her utterly and completely.

She didn't write any music for the next few days. She

lay on the filthy bed, coughing, spluttering and drinking. Occasionally, she hoiked up phlegm from the back of her throat and spat it into a bucket by the side of the bed. Zoltan, who had miraculously inherited his mother's musicianship, comforted her by continuing to play the piano for her.

There was another knock at the door of the caravan about three weeks later. The date was the third of February. Gladys Evans, looking even more frumpish than before, was accompanied by Judith Henderson, a senior social worker. A solicitor from the local council was also there. He was a frail-looking, yellow-faced man called Arthur Spink, who looked as if he had had about fifteen unsuccessful liver transplants. Added to the group was Detective Constable Bower whose eyes bored into Jessie's as if they were drilling holes in marble. He drove her backwards until she bumped into the wall of the caravan and fell.

Bower was the first to speak.

'Are you Mrs Jessie Lowther?'

'Yes.'

'There's a boy here, isn't there? Name of Zoltan.'

'He's my son.'

Judith Henderson took over from Bower.

'It is felt that you are unfit to look after this boy. You are a known drunkard and you have denied him the schooling which is required by law.'

'I teach him myself,' said Jessie.

'Would you please bring him forward and sit him at the table,' said Judith in a deadpan tone of voice.

Jessie led her son from his hiding place under the bed. 'Don't be frightened. They won't hurt you. They wouldn't dare,' she said lamely.

Zoltan was in tears. He knew that these people were going to take him away from his mother. Judith produced a notebook from her briefcase with a pen attached to it.

'Write a little about yourself, Zoltan. Keep it short. Just say what you do from day to day,' said Judith, adding, 'also write today's date at the top of the page.'

Zoltan had no idea what the date was. He drew ten sets of five lines on the page before him. He thought for a while before choosing a key and eventually decided on G major. Music cascaded from his brain on to the paper. He handed his work to Judith who was gruff and unsympathetic.

'That's all very well, dear, but I want you to write words.' Judith turned to the next page of her notebook.

Zoltan held the pen in his hand and stared at the menacing blank page facing him. He knew he had no idea how to read or write words. He didn't even know his alphabet. He stared at the page for a while and eventually drew a strange-looking squiggly shape which looked like a syphilis bacterium under a microscope. He got up and clung to Jessie.

'Don't let them take me away. Don't let them take me!'

Jessie wept as if her heart were broken. Her clothes, which she hadn't removed from her body for as far back as she could remember, stank. The smell of gin on her breath was even stronger than it had been when Gladys Evans had come to see her on her own.

'It has also been reported to us that you have been ill-treating this boy,' said Detective Constable Bower.

Zoltan became hysterical.

'That's not true. She's the kindest mother in the world!'

'That's all very touching but I am afraid we are going to have to take your son away and I have a warrant for this purpose,' said Detective Constable Bower.

Jessie composed herself.

'Before you take him away, may I have a word with him in private?'

'I suppose so, but keep it brief,' rasped Bower.

Jessie took Zoltan behind the screen where the bed was. She impressed on the seven-year-old boy the necessity of keeping safe the oblong wooden box, briefly repeated to him the Legend of the Zartak Knife and reminded him of the words, going into more detail about it on the parchment that the box contained, even though the boy could not even read English, let alone Hungarian.

'Guard this box with your life, Zoltan. It contains the parchment on which is written the Legend of the Zartak Knife in greater detail, as I've told you already. There would be no point in my keeping it because I haven't got long to live and it's possible that we will never meet again. When you grow up, take the parchment to a translation agency and ask them to translate the words on it into English. If you are still unable to read, ask someone to read it to you.'

The boy's weeping got totally out of control.

'You mustn't be afraid of a loved one's death, Zoltan,' said Jessie, adding, 'that person may die but the love for that person will live forever. Now let's have no more tears. Love is stronger than death,' Jessie added banally.

'OK, break it up,' snarled Bower.

The mother and child embraced and wept hysterically. Zoltan clutched the oblong wooden box to his chest.

It took the full force of Gladys, Judith, Spink and Detective Constable Bower to prize Jessie and Zoltan apart and drag the wretched, screaming boy to the van outside.

* * *

Jessie's shock over losing Zoltan didn't register straight away. For the next few weeks, a state of numbness took her over and she threw herself into writing the first movement of her sixth piano concerto in the relatively untaxing key of A minor. She presented it in an essentially Slavonic vernacular and vacillated from the slow, funereal and mournful to the fast, wild, frenzied climaxes, so typical of Slavonic dance music. She was subconsciously influenced by the Russian folk song, *Kasbek*, the song which started slowly and gradually gathered speed and which reminded her of Brigadier Poynings's sexual perversion, involving a pot of Vaseline and a walking stick. Her memory of this made her laugh a little.

During her period of numbness, she worked with extraordinary energy for most days, well into the night. She completed all four movements of her piano concerto in A minor within a week or two. This was the last concerto she would ever write.

It was then that her grief due to Zoltan's loss descended on her suddenly and with a vicious vengeance. She

151

abandoned her music and lay on her bed weeping, howling and screaming. Her beloved Labrador, Landy, who was only a puppy when she bought him, climbed onto her bed and licked the tears from her face.

She was drinking even more than before. Every morning, she was sick before drinking enough gin to make her fractionally less uncomfortable mentally, but her howling and weeping started again and faithful Landy carried on licking her face as before.

There came a time when she had no more tears to shed. It was early March when her grief changed to an increasingly blackening depression. She decided to leave Wales because long distance driving somehow helped her to take her mind off her misery. She consulted a map, intending to get as far away from her demons in Wales as possible. For no apparent reason, she decided to settle on a caravan site near Reading in Berkshire. At least she still had plenty of money.

She found a reliable and sympathetic drug dealer in Reading, a West Indian called Ned Wilson, who was nineteen years old and whom she liked and trusted. She and Wilson became good friends. They often drank in *The Bull's Horns*, a pub on the outskirts of Reading. Wilson did not use heroin himself and only sold it to help him to buy a fancy motorbike.

Approximately ten days passed. Jessie took some pleasure in playing her completed concerto in A minor. However, most of the time she lay on her back in a state of tearless, tormented apathy. With her blood dangerously saturated with gin and heroin, she yearned every day for death to come quickly. Jessie had just finished playing the last movement of her concerto in A minor a second time on the evening she left the caravan in order to kill herself. She left the score of the concerto in the piano rack, in the hope that it would one day be discovered. The date was the fifteenth of March. It was a Friday.

* * *

By the time the two women reached London, the saintly and forgiving Marcia's former peace of mind had changed to despair as she listened to Jessie's horrible story. She invited Jessie to stay in her large flat in London overlooking the Thames. She forced herself to appear cheerful, and to jolly Jessie along to make the last three days of her life as bearable as possible.

Jessie had bought enough heroin from Ned Wilson to last her for about a week, just in case her suicide attempt failed. When she was with Marcia, she gave herself an injection and drank a large quantity of gin which meant that for a full two hours her pitch-black spirits were relatively tolerable.

She timed her gin and heroin consumption to fit in with whatever entertainment Marcia had laid on for her. Marcia knew Jessie's tastes and it was she who decided what they would do to make Jessie as comfortable as possible.

On Saturday afternoon, Marcia took Jessie to see Stanley Kubrick's film, *A Clockwork Orange*, knowing that she would be stirred on seeing that even an evil delinquent can be roused by beautiful music. The violent scenes towards the beginning of the film to the accompaniment of Rossini's overture to *The Thieving Magpie*, and in particular, the famous

Billy Boy fight, presented more as a ballet than vicious, sadistic acts, cheered and delighted Jessie. When the main protagonist hit one of his fellow thugs on the thigh with his truncheon because he had made a disgusting noise while a professional blonde singer had gushed out with Beethoven's *Ode to Joy* in C major, Jessie was moved to tears.

However, as the film progressed to the harrowing scene depicting the main protagonist's receipt of aversion therapy in jail, her black mood descended on her again and Marcia had to take her out of the cinema and help her to get refuelled with gin and heroin.

It was Saturday evening. Following Jessie's further consumption of a colossal amount of gin and yet another heroin injection, the two young women attended a concert of Beethoven's Seventh Symphony at the Royal Albert Hall (where Keith Johnson had died of a massive heart attack.) The music had a disturbing effect on Jessie, although she felt roused and ennobled by it at the same time. She lay on the floor and bayed like a she-wolf that had just lost all her cubs, while startled members of the audience prodded her with their umbrellas and walking sticks and hissed for silence. Yet again, Marcia had to take Jessie out and wait for her to top herself up with gin and heroin.

It was Sunday just before lunch. It was the seventeenth of March, St Patrick's Day.

'Is there anything else you want to do at the moment?' asked Marcia kindly.

'I passionately want to visit an IRA pub. Today's St Patrick's Day.'

'Why an IRA pub?' asked Marcia.

'Because my grandmother, that is to say my foster mother's mother, was partly Irish on her mother's side. Sometimes she took me on her knee and sang Irish rebel songs. She stopped me from being sad while she did this. Do you know of an IRA pub?'

'Yes,' replied Marcia. 'There's an IRA pub in Willesden Lane, Kilburn, where they sing Irish rebel songs, particularly on St Patrick's Day. The pub is called Biddy Mulligan's.'

Marcia drove down Edgware Road and Kilburn High Road and finally reached Willesden Lane where Biddy Mulligan's was. (The pub was at the junction of Kilburn High Road and Willesden Lane.*) The two women went into the crowded pub. Marcia gave Jessie a ten pound note and told her what to get at the bar, namely two double whiskys and two double gin and tonics. Marcia did not choose to go to the bar herself, because she was embarrassed by her educated English accent. Instead, she sat down in a dark corner, and pulled from her bag a book by one of her favourite authors, the Marquis de Sade.† This was the most obscene book he had ever written and described

---

*The IRA pub is no longer at the junction of Kilburn High Road and Willesden Lane. It has been demolished.

†Marcia kept a set of the Marquis de Sade's works in her flat, partly to irritate her mother. She (Marcia) referred to de Sade as 'de Soggins'. The books she kept were in French. She kept *A Hundred and Twenty Days of Sodom* open with a bookmark where there was a particularly obscene passage describing: '*un vieux homme de quatre-vingt dix ans avec un petit garçon de six ans, chacun en train de chier dans la bouche de l'autre, et après avoir chié, ils ont avalé la merde et ensuite ils ont vomi d'une force ravissante.*' The author refrains from translating the above into English, but says her mother found the book open at the page describing the obscene passage, and said to the author, 'I'm so utterly shattered by your choice of reading matter, that all I want to do is take a cold shower!'

sexual perversions of the utmost depravity. It was entitled *A Hundred and Twenty Days of Sodom,* and it was in French. Suddenly, an IRA man leant over her shoulder.

'This man, the Marquiss de Sayed, did he ever do any good for Ireland?' he asked aggressively.

Marcia was terrified. She feared that the IRA man would recognize her educated English accent, so she used a bogus French accent.

'I'm afraid he never went to Ireland as he was in prison for most of his life, but if he had been a free man, I'm sure he would have buckled down and done his bit for the place,' she eventually managed to mutter.

Jessie then failed to distinguish herself by being copiously sick into an IRA fundraising bucket.

Marcia took her by the scruff of the neck, lied in her French accent that it was Jessie's birthday and dragged her outside into the street.

* * *

It was ten-thirty on Sunday night. Jessie had not lost her overpowering sex drive and suggested to Marcia that they go to the Hilton Hotel to pick up some men. Marcia didn't feel like doing this but she reluctantly agreed. The two women sat at the bar. Jessie was full of gin and heroin and was temporarily free of depression and Marcia, who was finding the whole situation increasingly unpleasant, decided to get systematically drunk.

* * *

156

Dub Booth was a wealthy American, who was born and raised in Texas. He had moved to Los Angeles where he became a high-ranking policeman. His wealth was boosted by the insurance money that he had gained after his wife's motoring accident. More than anything else on that cold, windy March evening, Dub Booth longed greedily for a woman and went down to the bar at the Hilton Hotel where he was staying.

The lift he used was empty apart from an Irishman called Sean McSharry whom he had met before in the hotel. McSharry used to work at menial jobs before he came into a vast inheritance after his aunt's death. He was on his way to the bar for the same reason as Dub Booth. He desperately wanted a woman.

Booth and McSharry occupied two bar stools next to Marcia and Jessie. Jessie stared lecherously at McSharry who was rugged, bearded and scruffy. McSharry was fixated by *nostalgie de la boue* and he found the stench of Jessie's filthy clothes alluring. This, combined with her white, emaciated feline face, sunken, bloodshot grey eyes and rancid, matted mane of jet-black hair, set his blood on fire.

Booth was well-built, suntanned and flabby. The pen of James Hadley Chase might have described him as having 'cop' written all over his face. He found Jessie repellent. He fixed his eyes on Marcia's pretty face and smart, bottle-green suit, and her stylish red hair pleased him. He was the first to break the silence.

'Say, do you mind if we buy you two ladies a couple of drinks?' he ventured.

Marcia introduced herself. 'We'd like that. My name's Marcia. This is my friend, Jessie but we all call her Cat Face because of her feline face. We were at school together. Today's her birthday so we aim to get drunk.'

Jessie asked for two double gin and tonics and Marcia said she wanted a double whisky and ice.

Booth and McSharry introduced themselves. McSharry was shy and a poor conversationalist. Booth was equally as handicapped but in a different way. He was a crashing and inveterate bore.

'My name is Booth, Dub Booth,' he said, addressing Marcia in a heavy Texan drawl. He added, 'I was once a cowboy. Now, I'm a goddam cop. It would give me pleasure to take you to mah room and show you mah hat, mah gun, mah boots and mah spurs.'

'I'd like that. Later perhaps,' said Marcia guardedly.

A silence followed. Jessie didn't feel like rambling pre-coital chatter. Marcia was dreading the following day, Monday, when Jessie was going to die. McSharry was too thick and shy to make intelligent conversation. Also, Booth was too obsessed by the need to talk about his hat, gun, boots and spurs to make intelligent conversation either. He repeated himself persistently, saying things he'd forgotten he'd said already.

'Back home in the States,' he began, 'I've got this doll called Marlene. When we dance, I like to hold her real close and she just *loves* the weight of mah gun.'

Marcia didn't comment but smiled sweetly. Because of the painful lack of flowing conversation, the four all got progressively drunk and stared at each other, giggling vacantly.

Booth broke the long silence.

'Here's something you guys ought to know. Back home in the States, I've got this doll called Marlene. When we dance, I like to hold her real close and she just *loves* the weight of mah gun.'

'You've told us that already!' snapped Jessie. 'I can tell you something a lot less boring than that. There were these two ancient Romans, lying side by side, on couches, stuffing their faces...'

Marcia got irritable as her nerves were fragile.

'For God's sake don't finish that joke, Cat Face!' she said, adding, 'I've heard it about fifty times before. It's a bloody awful joke.'

McSharry, who hadn't spoken for fifteen minutes, had shaken off his shyness with the help of a few double rums.

'I'll tell you a true story,' he said, adding, 'this time, it's about me. Some years ago, before I came into money, I was out of work so I went to a Job Centre.'

'"Where did you last work?" they asked. "In a mortuary," I said.

'"Is that so?" they said. "Why did you leave?"

'"I was fired," I said. "Why were you fired?" they asked.

'"For bunging the corpses down onto the slabs instead of laying 'em gently and after laying 'em down, for fucking 'em from behind," I replied.'*

*The author once met an Irishman at a bus stop in the nineteen seventies. The Irishman told her the above anecdote which was identical to the one accounted for here. It has to be noted that the author told the late Robert Maxwell the anecdote when she was inebriated, at which point Mr Maxwell said he was going upstairs to his bedroom where he wished to be given some hot, sweet tea.

Booth was sickened by the joke but Marcia, who had always had a taste for the macabre, roared with laughter with her mouth full of whisky. The whisky went down the wrong way and she spat some of it over the counter and coughed and spluttered.

'Are you a necrophiliac, Sean?' she asked eventually.

'A what?'

'You must know what a necrophiliac is. It's a person who screws the dead.'

'Contrary to what I was like earlier in my life, I prefer to screw the living because I like my balls to be sent back to me when I play tennis,' said McSharry vulgarly, his speech markedly slurred.

Marcia laughed again but Booth got angry.

'Aw, pack it in. You're making everyone sick. Let's turn in.'

'Cat Face, why don't you go up with Sean? I'll go with Dub. Besides, I want to see his hat, gun, boots and spurs,' said Marcia.

Jessie was not merely drunk. She was stupefied and her black spirits were completely camouflaged. She moved towards McSharry and fondled his private parts. Marcia raised her voice to her customary clipped military bark. The whisky had brought out a powerful exhibitionist streak in her and she yearned to be overheard by all the punters in the crowded bar.

'Listen, Cat Face, you fucking fool, when you go through the stages of seducing men, you don't kick off by stampeding down to their balls. You move a pawn first, not a couple of bloody knights!'

160

Jessie fell unconscious. McSharry carried her in the lift to his room on the tenth floor and had sex with her without her knowledge. Marcia accompanied Booth to his room but he was too drunk to perform sexually, which relieved Marcia because she didn't find him particularly attractive anyway. Instead, he told her one paralysingly boring anecdote after another, as well as making further repetitive references to the weight of his gun, until the boredom Marcia had to suffer was so acute that it reduced her to tears.

* * *

Monday came. It was the eighteenth of March. Marcia phoned *The Daily Mail* and told her boss that she had a heavy cold. It was raining hard and the sky was bleak and grey. This was the day Jessie would die. Once Jessie had loaded herself with gin and heroin, the two women got into Marcia's BMW and Jessie sat with her bottle of gin between her knees, looking moodily at the floor.

They travelled in silence down the M4 motorway from London to Bristol. Jessie produced a cassette of Russian folk songs with *Kasbek* among them, the one favoured by Brigadier Poynings, the eccentric who carried a cassette player and a jar of Vaseline in a plastic bag with him wherever he went. The Brigadier had given the tape to Jessie as a present in return for her services. She had kept the cassette in the inside pocket of her leather jacket. Marcia put it into the cassette player and wept silently. She felt as if she were mounting the steps of a scaffold although it was her friend, and not her, who was about to die.

Marcia pulled in to the side of the road just before the Clifton Suspension Bridge in Bristol. Beneath it stretched the Avon Gorge valley in which lay a dour expanse of mud and slime. On one side was a mass of craggy, jagged rocks.

Jessie sat in the passenger's seat and continued to look at the floor. Marcia took two swigs of whisky to steady her nerves and the whisky had never tasted so good or given her so much comfort as it did then. She got out from the driver's seat and opened the passenger's door, her head bowed like an obsequious butler.

'Come on, Cat Face. You've only got about two minutes to go.'

Marcia helped her to get out of the BMW. The two women walked slowly on to the bridge, their heads lowered to the ground, ignoring the sightseers who bumped into them, as well as the notice giving the phone number of the Samaritans.

The women stood side by side as they looked at the huge, sharp crags beneath them. The safely barrier was high and it looked impossible for anyone to be able to get over it.

'I don't think I'll be able to manage this. I've only got one good leg. The other one's wasted away due to so many fixes of heroin. You'll have to help me, Marcia,' said Jessie.

'I can't, Cat Face. I'd be charged with murder if I did. You must understand that,' said Marcia sternly.

'I'll get over the barrier somehow. I'll take it at a run,'

said Jessie, adding, 'I'm sure I'll be able to lift my own weight which is only about six stone. Thank you for being such a good friend, after I was so awful to you regarding your poem about the midwife who delivered Lenin, when we went to the Soviet Embassy that day.'

Marcia laughed briefly. She found displays of emotion distasteful for some reason which she could not comprehend. She forced herself not to cry. She hugged Jessie stiffly.

'Goodbye, dear Cat Face. I'm going back to the car. I'm not going to watch.'

As Marcia turned away, Jessie somehow managed to heave her weight over the high safety barrier. She nonsensically believed that the spirit of her father would be waiting for her in the valley, to explain whether he really had been shot dead or whether he had deserted her because he no longer wished to look after her. As her emaciated body bounced like a beach ball from crag to crag and just before her tortured spirit left her, she uttered a single word – '*Apa!*' which is the Hungarian for Daddy.

Marcia ran back to the car and drank as much whisky as she could hold. She abandoned the car due to her fear of being breathalysed. She ran down towards the gorge, using a winding path surrounded by bleak, leafless trees, until she reached the busy main road. She continued to run until she saw some police cars near where Jessie had fallen. A policeman got out of one of the cars and blocked her path.

'Keep away. There's been a dreadful accident,' said the policeman, his voice raised.

'I know. She was one of my closest friends.' Marcia became hysterical. 'I'll have to identify her at any rate. She's got no relations except for a seven-year-old son who I think is in an orphanage. That means I'll have to organize her funeral.'

'I understand all that, but you can't see her now. She ain't a pretty sight. Best to keep away, Miss, as I said.'

Marcia was fighting for breath, but her spirits were miraculously held together by the whisky which she had consumed.

'All right, I'll agree not to go and look. But please, just allow me to tell you a joke: there were these two ancient Romans, lying side by side on couches, stuffing their faces. One of them put a feather down his throat between courses and was sick over his friend who turned to him and shouted, "Oh, damn te!"'

The policeman roared with laughter but Marcia burst into floods of uncontrollable tears.

Epilogue

By the year two thousand and — , Hungary and her neighbouring eastern European states had long since become thriving capitalist countries. Zoltan Lowther, who had changed his name by deed poll to Zoltan Zartak, was a budding conductor, having started his career as a professional musician, after graduating with distinction from the Royal Academy of Music.

At the beginning of his career as a conductor, he had conducted a sizeable amount of his mother's work. Although he missed his mother profusely, when he was put in the orphanage, he soon settled down. He made friends with a lot of the other children and eventually even felt happy a lot of the time. He had become feisty, gutsy and extremely popular with the other children, particularly when he played the piano for them.

However, Geraldine, Jeanette's sister, visited him in the orphanage and claimed him as her adopted son when he was nine years old. It was Marcia who told Geraldine where Zoltan was. A deep-rooted bond developed between Zoltan and Geraldine. She raised him herself, taught him to read and write English, and made him work so hard, with the aid of a strict governess, that he passed his Common Entrance exam, went to Eton where he excelled in music, and won a scholarship to the Royal Academy of Music, like his mother.

Zoltan remained loyal to Jessie throughout his life but did not inherit her self-destructive rebelliousness, melancholia, drunkenness or heroin addiction. He was industrious and ambitious. He inherited dogged and resilient ruthlessness from his maternal grandfather, Lazlo Zartak. Like his mother, he closely resembled him in looks with his jet-black hair, and large grey eyes.

It was in two thousand and — that Zoltan travelled to Budapest to attend an auction which was held in a former post office. This had become a hall of remembrance to the victims of communist rule. Weapons removed from the hands of rebels trying to cross frontiers to the west were being sold. Among these was the legendary Zartak Knife with its intricately engraved blade and its ivory handle. Zoltan had studied the English translation of the parchment in the box which his mother had given him, and he yearned to repossess the Zartak Knife. He made a bid for it and bought it for the post-inflation equivalent of a hundred thousand pounds.

Zoltan returned to London where Jessie had been buried in an obscure cemetery by Marcia, who had died two years after Jessie died, of uterine cancer. Zoltan had his mother's body exhumed and when her coffin had been prized open, he placed the Zartak Knife underneath her skeletal hands and kissed her skull, round which he laid a plethora of lilies. He placed white orchids round her body which he had taken to Hungary to be buried somewhere in the dense wood at the frontier between Hungary and Austria where Lazlo Zartak had been shot dead.

In the wood, Zoltan commissioned the building of a white, marble sepulchre which could be entered by a doorless opening. A marble effigy of Jessie lay within it, showing her former striking feline face, before her body had been destroyed by gin and heroin. This would be Jessie's tomb.

Zoltan entered the sepulchre and kissed his mother's marble face and her serenely clasped marble hands. On the pedestal on which her sculpted statue lay, her own words to her son translated into Hungarian were engraved: *Love is stronger than death.* Underneath, in smaller letters, was written (also in Hungarian): *In devoted memory of Rosa Zartak, the brilliant musician and composer, otherwise known as Jessie Lowther who was nicknamed 'Cat Face' by her friends. May her tortured soul find rest.*

Within the next few months, Zoltan, who had once only been well-known in Britain, became internationally famous as a conductor. Within a year, he dined at the tables of presidents, prime ministers and kings.

He married an American violinist called Gerry-Beth Hardesty who was kind, rich, beautiful and amusing as well as mentally stable.

When Zoltan and Gerry-Beth first met, they were sitting next to each other at a dinner at the White House.

'How did you become so rich and famous so quickly?' asked Gerry-Beth.

After dinner, Zoltan took her to his five-star hotel in Washington. While they were in bed, he familiarized her with the Legend of the Zartak Knife, as described in greater detail by an English translation of the words on the parchment contained in the oblong wooden box which he always kept with him.

Zoltan proposed to Gerry-Beth and later married her. They settled in a large house in Mayfair, in London, and were able to buy equally as large houses in Budapest, San Francisco, Rome, Washington and Paris. Gerry-Beth gave birth to three daughters followed by a son. The daughters were called Rosa, Marcia and Geraldine. They all went into the music business and excelled. Their younger brother, Lazlo, became a successful and brilliant barrister who never lost a case.

The legendary Zartak Knife remains in Jessie's tomb, clasped by her skeletal hands.